Inn The Spirit of Legends

SPIRIT OF TEXAS COZY MYSTERIES, BOOK 1

BECKI WILLIS

Clear Creek Publishing

Publisher's Note: This is a work of fiction. Names, characters, places, and incidents are a product of the author's imagination. Locales and public names are sometimes used for atmospheric purposes. Any resemblance to actual people, living or dead, or to businesses, companies, events, institutions, or locales is completely coincidental.

Cover Design by dienel96
Editing by SJS Editorial Services
Book Layout © 2017 BookDesignTemplates.com

Inn the Spirit of Legends/ **Becki Willis** -- 1st ed.
ISBN 978-1-947686-11-3

Books by Becki Willis

Forgotten Boxes
Tangible Spirits
He Kills Me, He Kills Me Not
The Mirror Series
        The Girl from Her Mirror
        Mirror, Mirror on Her Wall
        Light from Her Mirror
The Sisters, Texas Mystery Series
        Chicken Scratch – Book 1
        When the Stars Fall – Book 2
        Stipulations & Complications – Book 3
        Home Again: Starting Over – Book 4
        Genny's Ballad – Book 5
        Christmas In The Sisters – Book 6
Spirits of Texas Cozy Mysteries
        Inn the Spirit of Legends – Book 1

Dedicated to Roger:
My best friend, biggest supporter, and my partner in life for
the past thirty-odd years. And counting.

CONTENTS

CHAPTER 1

"Lookie here, little brother." The man jabbed a stubby finger at the newspaper article, leaving a greasy smear across the print. He licked the last bit of barbecue sauce from his thumb and sat back to cackle in glee. "We done hit pay-dirt. That old broad finally died. Now's our chance to do some snoopin'."

His brother peered over his shoulder, squinting his eyes into beady slits. "What's it say?"

"Read it for yourself."

He patted at empty pockets. "Don't have my glasses on me."

"Don't tell me you lost them," the older brother huffed. "Again."

"I didn't exactly *lose* them. It's more like I misplaced them." His voice came out with a whine. "Just tell me what it says."

"It says the old hag finally croaked and they put the property up for sale. Auctioned it off, don't you know. For the first time in over one hundred and sixty-five years, the town of Hannah, Texas is no longer controlled by the Hannah clan. No clan, no curse." He thumped the newsprint in satisfaction and clicked his tongue with a distinct pop. "If that ain't an invitation to come a callin', I don't know what is."

Greed lit both men's eyes. The younger man let out a whoop. "Think it's still there? Think we'll find it, just like our granddaddy always said? He said the only copy of the treasure map was in that old inn."

"One way to find out." The man opened a drawer on the side table and pulled out a pistol. "Looks like you and me is going to Texas, little brother."

CHAPTER 2

She was already five minutes late for her meeting.

After plugging the coordinates into her GPS and promptly loosing signal, Hannah Duncan discovered the higher peaks of the Balcones Escarpment played havoc with satellite positioning and cell phone service. She had left the main highway some forty-five minutes ago, wandered around through a series of turns and curves, traversed rugged hills and flowing streams, and somehow managed to come out almost in the exact same spot from where she started. Still nowhere near where she needed to be.

Hannah glanced again at the time. The only number she had for the lawyer was at his office, where an answering machine picked up the call. Without a cell number, she had no way to warn him she was running late. Her only choice was to drive fast and hope he was a patient man.

She took a left onto the blacktop ribbon and sped along its patched path, taking little time to appreciate the scenic landscape. Rocky hills blended into hayfields. Elaborate new homes intermingled with old stone houses and weathered barns. Fields alternated with goats or cattle. The area was known for its whitetail deer and spotted axis. Hannah enjoyed looking at the wildlife as much as anyone, but she hoped the deer stayed on their side of the fence and off the narrow two-lane road.

"Obviously, I turned way too early," she chastised herself. "By now, though, I should be getting close..." She glanced down at her phone for directions, completely missing one of the more useful landmarks on her left. She sailed on down the road until she spotted a sign on the right.

"Great," Hannah muttered, "now I've gone too far!" She remembered the email directing her to turn between the Town Loop and Uptown Luckenbach. With a low growl of frustration, Hannah whipped the car around and grumbled aloud, "You'd think if it was famous enough to have its own song, you'd at least be able to see it on the side of the road."

She slowed the car to a crawl, so she didn't miss her turn. Again. At this rate, she'd be lucky to make it by nightfall. "Please be waiting on me," she begged the absent attorney. "Don't let me have come all this way for nothing." According to her directions, she still had several more miles to go, and this road was even narrower, and quite winding. It was silly, she knew, because the man couldn't hear her, but she repeated the plea, this time with extra zeal.

Hannah watched her speedometer and clocked the precise mileage given in the directions. The GPS gods smiled upon her and allowed a signal through, directing her to her final turn. She made a left, crossing over a rocky creek bed and following the graveled path up a steep embankment. The road was well maintained but bumpy. Atop the rocky hill, she saw the first promise of the town, nestled there in a grove of trees and bramble.

"Ah, a gated community." She smirked, driving beneath an ornate iron arch bearing the town's name in vintage lettering.

So this was Hannah, Texas.

It reminded her of a Hollywood movie set for an old western. The graveled road forked around a large grassy area that boasted a trio of massive old live oaks, met up again on the far side, and meandered its way into the sunset... or to at least as far as the tree line. A collection of old, weathered buildings—some eight or so in all, in various degrees of disrepair—loosely clustered around either fork of the road.

Hannah spotted a pickup truck parked near the largest of the buildings and felt a surge of relief. Thank heavens, the lawyer had waited! Maybe there was something to telepathic messaging, after all. She edged her sporty little car up next to the truck, tugged sunglasses into place, and braced for the Texas heat.

A man emerged from the weathered structure as she hurried from her car. A crooked sign above the door identified it as the *Stagecoach Stop*. An official state historical marker identified it as important.

With a stab of disappointment, Hannah realized this wasn't the lawyer, after all.

She disqualified him on two accounts: age and dress. Not only was he too young—hardly older than she was, it would seem—but his clothes were much too casual. Even though his jeans and pale-blue western shirt were neatly starched and pressed, his shirt was open at the collar, no tie in sight, his boots dusty and scuffed. Definitely not lawyer attire.

He thrust out a hand and smiled, but the effort looked strained. "Hannah Duncan?"

"Yes, I'm Hannah," she acknowledged, accepting his brisk handshake. She glanced around for sight of someone else. "I was supposed to meet the attorney here at one, but I'm afraid I took a wrong turn. Have I missed him?"

"No, you're fine."

She waited for him to expand on his statement. Perhaps he would offer to take her inside and make introductions. Explain that the lawyer was in one of the other buildings. That he was answering the call of nature and would be with them shortly. Something. Anything.

Instead, the man simply stood there, his tight expression unreadable.

Hannah finally gave up and asked, "Where is he?" Her expression hinted at exasperation.

The man did something with his brows, a subtle lift that gave him a superior air. It irritated Hannah, knowing she chose that exact moment to realize how attractive he was. A good six feet tall, with a trim, muscular build and a nice head of black hair. A perfect, aquiline nose, with nostrils flared just enough to signal his impatience.

"*I* am Walker Jacoby," he informed her sharply. "Attorney at law, at your service." He gave a half bow, the gesture mocking.

Her eyes flew over him again, taking in the long, jean-encased legs, the cowhide belt and shiny buckle, the hint of curly chest hair peeking over the top buttons of his monogrammed shirt. She could picture him as a rodeo champion. A country music star. Some sort of western show promoter. A drugstore cowboy wannabe. But she couldn't quite imagine him as an attorney.

His stiff smile turned into a smirk. "Is there a problem, Ms. Duncan?"

"You're an attorney?" The question popped out before she could censure it.

"That's what it says on my diploma." He appeared suitably perturbed as he scowled. "Is this going to be a problem? Perhaps I should speak with Mr. Duncan."

Fire flashed in Hannah's eyes, dancing blue flames that threatened to spark at any moment. Despite the heat building in her pointed glare, her voice was cold. Each word fell like a shard of ice from her tongue. "What a disturbingly chauvinistic thing to say. There isn't a *Mister* Duncan, and even if there were, I hardly need a man to step in and speak for me. Do I make myself clear, Mr. Jacoby?" She couldn't help but offer her own sneer. "Or shall I explain that to *Mrs.* Jacoby?"

Something flickered in his own eyes, which were a much paler shade of blue than her own. That something could have been anger, could have been amusement. Hannah didn't bother to dwell on his eyes. She had decided the man wasn't so attractive, after all.

"No need," he assured her. "Mrs. Jacoby is of the same opinion."

So, the cad was married. *Poor woman*, Hannah thought of his wife.

"And if there's no Mr. Duncan," he added smugly, "we might have a problem. He's the one who actually made the purchase."

Understanding dawned in Hannah's eyes, dousing the flame. "You were referring to my uncle, Joseph Duncan." She had the grace to look embarrassed. He hadn't been patronizing her, after all.

Or had he? Something about his smug look suggested he might think men were superior to women, at least when handling legal matters.

"My uncle has... peculiar... tastes in gift giving, to say the least. The purchase was my birthday gift. As benefactor of that gift, I am the sole person you will be dealing with, Mr. Jacoby."

He rocked back on his heels and assured her, "Hey, not a problem for me. You were the one who seemed to be struggling with the concept of working with me."

"Not at all," she snapped. "I was merely surprised by your informality. Most lawyers I know wear a suit and tie when meeting with a client, particularly for the first time."

"Do you visit the Hill Country often, Ms. Duncan?"

"No," she admitted. "Other than going to San Antonio twice and the State Capitol in Austin once, this is actually my first time."

He brushed away her statement with a wave of his hand. "Neither city is considered within the boundaries of the Hill Country," he said. "But you will soon notice that formalities, and ties, are in short supply around here." With a sudden smile that looked almost genuine, he asked, "So, shall we get down to business, Ms. Duncan?"

Too bad, the smile was also very attractive.

"You might as well call me Hannah," she said with a hint of resignation. "And yes, please. I'd like to know what couldn't be discussed over the phone or by email."

It was his turn to sigh. "Quite a bit, to be honest. Why don't we start with a tour? Then we can go inside and talk brass tacks."

Something about the way he said it all made Hannah uncomfortable. She sensed he was hiding something from her. But what could it be? A tax lien on the property? A disputed property line?

No, she reasoned, neither scenario was plausible. That's what title searches and surveys were for, and JoeJoe was smart enough to insist on both before making a purchase, even for a fluke gift.

Perhaps there was a cemetery on the property, and he wasn't sure how she would take the news. Or perhaps the previous owner died here. Both thoughts were a bit creepy, but neither were deal breakers.

Not one to beat around the bush, Hannah stood her ground. "If you don't mind, I'd prefer to nail those tacks down, first thing."

Her directness surprised him, but he nodded in agreement and gestured toward the old inn. "We'll be more comfortable inside." As they started toward the front steps, he asked, "What do you know about your little town, Ms.—Hannah?"

"Nothing," she readily admitted. "Not a thing, other than the fact we share a name."

"The community was founded by Ezekiel Hannah in 1851, where he and his wife operated a stagecoach stop for several years. The inn is original to the property and built by Ezekiel Hannah and Henry Anheim in about 1853. Watch your step here on the entry."

He held the door open and allowed her to enter first. As she passed by him, Hannah got a whiff of something outdoorsy and decidedly male. The entryway they stepped into felt crowded, especially when he leaned close and pushed open the second door. There was no denying the little zing of electricity radiating from the man like a live current.

He's married, she reminded herself in a singsong voice. He didn't wear a ring, but he was definitely off limits. Besides, his holier-than-thou attitude would be a deal breaker, even if his wife weren't. Which she was. Hannah held high regards for the institution of marriage, even though she had no plans of it for herself, anytime soon.

"I came out earlier and opened up the place, but it's still a little stuffy inside," he apologized. He waved a hand to the room beyond. "Welcome to the *Spirits of Texas Inn*."

A long room ran the breadth of the building, with a limestone fireplace holding reign on either end. A collection of mismatched armchairs guarded the hearth on the left; a dozen or so dining tables and chairs scattered across the expanse to the right. Straight ahead was the front desk.

It reminded Hannah of something from a western movie, like an old bank teller's cage, but without the bars. Elaborate fretwork and hand-carved details gave the space distinction and matched the oak support pillars standing about the room like stoic sentries. The long check-in counter even came with a vintage grid to hold room keys and messages.

"How quaint," she murmured, completely underwhelmed.

The hardwood floors looked original, bearing the scars and scuffs of a century past. The walls were simple shiplap, the raw hewn lumber long since darkened with age. Everything in the room was outdated, from the frilly white eyelet curtains to the brass-plated light fixtures.

Despite the dowdy appearance now a decade or three out of vogue, something about the room spoke to Hannah. It seemed to have a presence. Or, she mused, perhaps it was that it had a *past*. This was history, plain and raw. Very plain, very raw, but there was still something about it...

"Let's have a seat," the lawyer suggested, gesturing to a table strewn with paperwork. He pulled out a straight-back chair and waited for Hannah to be seated before he settled in the chair directly across from her.

"Though never incorporated," he explained, "what started as a stagecoach shop and livery soon grew into quite a busy little town. At one time, there were as many as twenty or so families living here. There was a blacksmith, general store, two saloons, one church, and a gristmill. Eventually, the only thing left of the town was the inn, which was actually quite prosperous. For over one hundred and sixty-five years, and through five generations, a member of the Hannah family has lived here and kept the inn in operation."

"So how did the town end up in an auction?"

"The last owner, Wilhelmina Hannah, never married. As the last descendant of Ezekiel and Elsa Hannah, she was sole heir to the property. When she died last year at the age of eighty-seven, she left very specific instructions about the handling of her estate. It was her wish for the town to be sold at auction."

Hannah's brow puckered as she contemplated his words. "That seems a bit odd."

"There's more."

At his cautious tone, her eyes flew up to meet his.

"There's stipulations, aren't there?" Hannah realized. She jumped up to restlessly pace near the table. "That's just like JoeJoe. He didn't read the fine print, did he?" Her tone dared him to contradict her, but she gave him no opportunity. Wheeling around on her heels, she continued with her rant. "He got caught up in the excitement of bidding, and no telling what God-awful price he ended up paying. JoeJoe loves a good competition. A man like my uncle, God love him, can't be bothered with details, not when he can buy himself the win."

"Please, sit down." The attorney's tone was borderline testy, making it more of a command than a request. He reached for a folder from the table. "I have no idea which of the conditions your uncle may or may not have bothered with, but yes, there were conditions listed. The main requirement is that the inn must remain open and operational."

"What? Are you *kidding me*?"

In contrast to her incredulous cry, Walker Jacoby's voice remained quiet and oddly patient. "There is no need to yell, Miss Duncan. And yes, you heard me correctly. The inn is to remain in business."

Hannah's head whipped around as she surveyed the room. A lock of dark hair slung into her gaping mouth, but she hardly noticed. She did notice, however, that despite its ancient decor, the inn was tidy and well kept.

But operational? She had her doubts.

She spat out the mouthful of ebony curls. "People still stay here?" she asked incredulously.

"Actually, yes. There are a handful of loyal customers who continue to return here, year after year."

"But... who's been taking care of them?"

"Sadie and Fred Tanner are the caretakers, and the only other residents of the town. They took care of the inn, as well as the animals and the gardens, long before Miss Wilhelmina died."

Her head began to spin. Of all the oddball gifts her uncle had given her over the years, this was the most ridiculous yet. "Animals?"

"You also own a small herd of goats, five head of cattle, several laying hens, one rooster, six horses, and assorted ducks and geese." He made the announcement in a gleeful voice as he opened the folder and read from one of the papers inside.

Thank goodness, he had insisted she sit back down. Her knees never would have held her. "G—G—Goats?"

The look on her face obviously amused him. "Don't forget the cattle. Which happens to include two good Guernsey milk cows, so serving fresh milk to your guests is never a problem."

"F—Fr—Fresh milk?"

"Are you going to repeat everything I say? Because there are quite a few things we need to go over this afternoon, and saying them just once will take long enough."

Hannah closed her eyes and concentrated on taking deep, even breaths. She owned goats and chickens. And milk cows.

Holy boomtown, JoeJoe has turned me into a farmer! She had a ridiculous image of herself in a pair of overalls and a floppy straw hat, munching on a piece of straw.

Fighting off a wave of hysteria, Hannah forced herself to remain calm. She opened her eyes and made a guess. "You're telling me I have to reimburse the Tanners?" She vaguely wondered if she could pay them in eggs and fresh milk. Maybe a nice side of beef.

Much to her relief, the lawyer shook his head. "Not at all." He flashed a smile that was charming enough to penetrate her fogged brain. "You were right. Your uncle did pay a God-awful price to win that auction. Luckily for you, the proceeds went into a trust for the property. Along with money Miss Wilhelmina put into it, you will be able to keep the inn running for years to come. Have no fear, the Tanners have already been compensated for all their hard work."

"Wait." She threw up both palms and waved them defensively, as if to stop the onslaught of his words. "Wait, wait,

wait. I have no intentions of keeping this inn running, Mr. Jacoby."

"Please, call me Walker." Now that she was in a full-out panic, his demeanor had changed dramatically. Despite his earlier stiffness, he seemed completely relaxed now. Almost jovial.

"I have no intentions of keeping this inn running, *Walker*." Changing the name didn't change her tone. It was still vehement. "I'm not an innkeeper. I don't *want* to be an innkeeper. My life is in Houston."

"Oh? What is it you do in Houston? Where do you work?" There was an edge in his voice. A slight tilt of his dark head.

He knows good and well I have no job, she fumed.

Hannah lifted her chin. "I am an investment analyst. I am currently looking for new employment, as I think you well know."

He appreciated her sharp retort, if the light in his eyes was any indication. Hannah ignored the glimmer, wishing she could as easily ignore the man.

"Did I mention the arrangement comes with a salary, as well as a very generous bonus?"

She sat up straighter in her seat, trying not to look as interested as she felt. She picked at a thread on her linen walking shorts. "Oh?" she asked coolly.

"The trust provides a generous yearly budget for the inn. This allows for operational expenses, including a salary for the new owner." He took another paper from the file and slid it across the table for her inspection.

Okay, not a fortune, but decent. Particularly if I have no rent, no utility bills.

When she realized the direction of her thoughts, she gave herself a stern and visible shake.

Walker bit back a grin. It was as if he could read her very thoughts. "Naturally, you would be living here at the inn." His tone suggested it might be a thought that hadn't yet occurred to her, but the glint in his blue eyes said differently. "Most of your living expenses would be covered."

She hoped she sounded suitably nonchalant. "Hmm. I suppose that would help. *If* I were interested."

"From a monetary perspective, there is no reason the inn cannot be successful. No mortgage, no property taxes, no monthly utility bills. Even if you have no experience running an inn, you must admit, it's an intriguing offer. Most every dime you make would be profit."

She leaned in a bit closer, drawn to the possibilities.

"Of course, you would need to put the money back into the business," he went on to say. "Miss Wilhelmina and I worked out a very comprehensive budget that hinges on re-investing in the trust. Even using a modest income projection and an overly aggressive rate of inflation, I feel confident the inn can maintain a fully-funded operational budget for years to come."

"Why—Why would she do that? Why would she set aside all that money? It would have to be a literal fortune, to fund all the bills for several years."

The attorney flashed a disarming smile. With a smile like that, she could easily forget about his rakish personality and his invisible wedding ring. "Don't forget your uncle's very generous donation to the cause. As for the reason, it's really quite simple. Miss Wilhelmina loved the town of Hannah and the *Spirits of Texas Inn.* She dedicated her life to keeping both alive."

Hannah glanced out the window, to the ghost of a town outside. "Well, I'm not so sure she kept the *town* alive..."

"But she kept its chances alive, and that's almost as important. There are many possibilities for a town like this. The purpose of the trust is to ensure that at least some of those possibilities are explored."

One corner of Hannah's mouth dipped south. "You're telling me there are more conditions."

In answer, he pulled out another sheet of paper.

He went over a list of a dozen do's and don'ts. Although Hannah didn't understand the logic behind some, none were so outlandish or so unreasonable that she balked. *If* she were interested, she could work with the conditions he listed.

Still, her head spun with the enormity of it all. Her, an inn owner? And not just any inn. An inn in the middle of nowhere. An inn in dire need of updating.

Breaking free of the whirlwind in her head, she practically snapped, "I believe you mentioned a bonus?"

His smile revealed a row of pearly white teeth. "Ah, I wondered when you would remember that. Yes, there are two very generous bonuses, actually. The second bonus wasn't mentioned in the conditions of the sale. It is a 'bonus' bonus, you might say. On the first anniversary of your purchase, if three simple conditions have been met, you will receive a bonus check of five thousand dollars, to do with as you please. No stipulations."

Her eyes widened when she heard the amount, then narrowed in suspicion. "And what are these three conditions?"

"One, the inn must still be in business. Two, you must have a solid business plan in place. And three, you must continue to accommodate Miss Wilhelmina's special guests."

"None of those sound too difficult," Hannah mused. "Actually, it sounds like an easy five thousand dollars."

He did that thing with his eyebrows again. "*If* you meet the condition of the first bonus."

"Which is?"

"You must remain on the property, without leaving, for the first thirty days after taking over."

She stared at him in surprise. "You mean... like... a prisoner?"

"No bars," he assured her with his most charming smile. "But no leaving."

"No leaving the inn, or no leaving the town?" she clarified.

"The town, as defined by the fence surrounding the property. You are free to move about at your leisure, but you aren't allowed to venture further than the gates."

"Not even to buy groceries?"

"I will be happy to bring whatever you need."

"What if I get sick and need a doctor?"

"We have a local doctor who can make house calls, if needed." He frowned and gave her a thorough perusal. "You're not suffering from an illness I should know about, are you?"

"No, of course not. And even if I were, you wouldn't need to know about it. My health is none of your concern," she sniffed.

"Actually, it is. It is my responsibility to carry out the terms of both the purchase and of Miss Wilhelmina's will. If you aren't fit to meet the conditions of either, it is important I know so now."

"I am completely healthy, Mr. Jacoby."

"Walker," he reminded her. "We will be working closely with one another, Hannah. We might as well be on friendly terms."

She eyed him with suspicion. "Why will we be working together? And why does she have this ridiculous stipulation in the terms?"

"I'm afraid I cannot speak on the behalf of Miss Wilhelmina, at least in that regard. I merely carry out her wishes. And it was her wish I act as trustee and financial planner for the trust."

"So, you control the money."

"That is one way of saying it, yes."

Hannah let his words soak in before she finally gave a shake of her dark head. "I still don't understand. Why would I agree to stay here for thirty days without stepping foot off the property?"

"Because if you fail to meet this one non-negotiable term of sale, the entire deal becomes null and void." He saw the hopeful expression that crossed her face. "That God-awful price your uncle paid, as you so aptly put it, would be forfeited. Believe me, Hannah, you don't want that to happen."

"But—but—!" she sputtered in outrage before she found her voice. "You're telling me that unless I agree to this ridiculous farce of a deal, my uncle losses his money? Unbelievable! And most likely illegal! That's—That's extortion!"

"The condition of the deal was clearly and visibly displayed on the auction site. Your uncle agreed to all terms before he placed his first bid."

"My uncle was too caught up in the thrill of bidding to bother with the details!"

"Your uncle is a shrewd businessman, Hannah. He knows not to enter into a legally binding contract without reading the fine print."

"And how do you know?" she snapped.

"I give the man credit for as much. At any rate, he initialed the stipulation when signing the papers. Like it or not, your uncle knew what was at stake before agreeing to purchase the property."

She wanted to protest, but what could she say? He was right, of course. JoeJoe wasn't only an adult who was responsible for his own actions, but he was an astute businessman. If he failed to read the contract, that was on him.

A niggling of suspicion wormed into her thoughts. Is that why he had urged her to come? He would be out of the country. For at least thirty days. By the time he returned, the screaming and kicking phase of her tantrum would be over.

"This is so like JoeJoe," she muttered beneath her breath.

Walker Jacoby allowed her time to process all she had learned. He waited patiently as an array of emotions passed over her face, the strongest of which included anger, resentment, irritation, and, at last, resignation. She took a deep breath, squared her shoulders, and looked him in the eye.

"I suppose the first bonus is the fact that, if I stay the thirty days, my uncle doesn't forfeit his money?"

"The bonus is that if you stay, you get access to the trust, and ensure operational expenses for the foreseeable future."

"Controlled by you, of course," she added coolly.

He arched his brows in answer, a gesture she was quickly coming to detest. "It also includes a very generous budget for whatever updates you might want to make."

Her eyes inadvertently darted around the room, seeing a dozen things that needed doing. It would take a small fortune to bring this one room, alone, up to the standards she was accustomed to.

He deftly slid another piece of paper her way. "I did mention that it was quite generous, didn't I?"

Eyes widening when she saw the amount, Hannah asked, "What did this woman do for a living, rob banks?"

"She was an innkeeper, Hannah."

"There is no way keeping an inn, particularly this one, could make her that much money!" Hannah tapped the figure shown on the paper.

"Miss Wilhelmina was a sharp businesswoman. You would be wise to study her business plan."

Hannah stood from the chair and dared to venture around, arms crossed over her queasy stomach as she studied the room. "You mentioned loyal guests."

"Yes. If you consult your reservations, you'll find you have several bookings for June. That should give you plenty of time to settle in, complete your thirty-day challenge, and start working on the changes you'd like to make."

"You make it sound so simple..."

He gave her that smile again, that one that made her forget his more obnoxious qualities. "Unless you have a job or a significant other waiting for you in Houston, it really is quite simple. This is your town now, Hannah. You can move in immediately. The sooner you start, the sooner you earn those bonuses."

She could think of thousands of reasons why his offer made sense. Enough money for renovations. A trust to ensure her business success. Another five thousand reasons—money to do with as she pleased—at the end of one year.

For the life of her, she couldn't think of a single reason to refuse, not even the fact she knew nothing about running an inn.

"I—I'll consider it," she said.

"I need your answer by the end of the day tomorrow."

"What?" she cried, throwing her hands wide. "That's insane!"

"There is specific language in the will," he explained, "as to expiration dates for all bonuses. Your uncle made the purchase almost six months ago. You came just in the nick of time."

Hannah ignored the reproachful tone in his voice. She was known for over-thinking every situation. She loved to make lists. She had even been known to make a chart or two, to better analyze those lists. JoeJoe forever teased her about her obsession with pondering every possibility before making a decision. He claimed she never did anything spontaneous.

Well, JoeJoe was *wrong.*

Marching back to the table, her blue eyes blazed with a defiance the lawyer couldn't possibly understand.

"Fine. I accept. Is there something I need to sign?"

He pulled out the thickest of the files and opened it. "As a matter of fact," his smile was enigmatic, "there is."

CHAPTER 3

Once the papers were signed, Walker handed her a ring of keys.

"I'd like to stay and show you around the property," he said, "but I have to get back to the office. I can come back this evening, if you like."

"When does the imprisonment begin?" she asked sardonically. "Am I allowed to at least go grocery shopping?"

"Certainly. Let's say we start your thirty-day period tomorrow morning, at promptly eight o'clock. I'll bring a paper to sign."

"Of course you will. My hand is still cramping from all your other papers," she complained.

"There's a lot involved in owning your own town."

"There's also no need to delay the inevitable. My imprisonment may as well start at eight tonight."

He ignored her cross attitude and merely nodded. "As you wish."

"So, when do I get to meet the caretakers?"

"When they return from vacation. About two weeks from now."

"Wait. I'll be here, all alone?" she clarified.

"I'll drop in at least twice a day."

"To spy on me."

"And to help you with anything you need," he assured her. "I'll even volunteer to help you feed the animals. How does that sound?"

"I have to feed them?" Her voice rose in something close to hysteria.

"They're living animals, Hannah. They require food and water."

"Yes, but... they can't just scrounge around for it? This is the country. Surely they can fend for themselves out here."

He gave her a stern look. "I'll be back around six. Will that give you time to do your grocery shopping?"

"I think so. As soon as I find the nearest town with a grocery store."

He pointed opposite the way she had come. "Fredericksburg, ten miles that way." His light-blue eyes grazed over her. "You might want to pick up some suitable attire."

"What's wrong with my attire?" she asked. She wore a pair of fashionable shorts and a silk blouse, with sandals.

His eyes were dancing. "Nothing. You look like you just drove in from Houston."

"I did."

"Exactly. But you're in Hannah now. As you pointed out, this is the country. You'll need work clothes. I think you'll be more comfortable in jeans and tees. And boots," he added. "The kind without suede and five-inch heels."

She gave him a withering look. "Suede is so out of season."

"A good pair of leather boots never goes out of style. I recommend *Clancy's Western Wear*, right on Main."

"Let's get back to the caretakers... Can't you call them and ask them to come back any sooner?"

"They haven't had a vacation in three years, Hannah. They're visiting family in Florida and then taking a cruise."

"But I can't stay here all alone! I don't know the first thing about staying in the country."

"It's no different from staying in the city. You get up every morning, do whatever it is you need to do, eat, sleep, and start all over again the next day."

"It's totally different!" she protested. "For one thing, there's no policemen here."

"Sure there are. We have a very capable sheriff's department with several well-qualified and helpful deputies at your service."

"Not on every corner, there's not!"

"Because there's not a criminal on every corner," he pointed out. "Believe me, you're safer here than you are in the city. Our crime rate is impressively low."

"There are no streetlights!"

"True. But you can see the stars here. And I can bring you flashlights and lanterns." When he wasn't spouting legal jargon, his tone was much more affable. Hannah suspected he might be laughing at her.

"You honestly expect me to stay here, all alone, out here in the middle of nowhere?" Her voice edged upward with a hint of hysteria.

"Why? Are you scared?" Judging from his tone, it sounded as if he thought the notion preposterous.

Hannah's reply was quick and honest. "Terrified!"

With a nervous gulp, her eyes darted around the large, airy room. She couldn't imagine spending an entire night here. Alone. In the dark.

A thoughtful expression crossed the attorney's handsome face. His brows puckered in concern. "Let me consult the terms and conditions. I may have an idea," he offered.

Not trusting herself to speak, Hannah nodded. Now wasn't the time to smart off and say something to alienate him, not if he could offer a solution to her staying here alone.

He gathered his files and binders, and stuffed them into a crate. Hoisting it up like it weighed no more than a feather, he asked, "So, I'll meet you here at six this evening?"

Her answer escaped on a resigned sigh. "Yes."

"I'll see myself out then. Feel free to explore on your own." He tossed the last over his shoulder, but he paused at the threshold with an afterthought. "Oh, and if you see a big white dog, his name is Leroy."

She had immediate visions of a fanged beast with glowing eyes. "He's not dangerous, is he?"

The lawyer laughed. "Only if you get in the way of his wagging tail and his adoring tongue."

Instead of being relieved, Hannah had a new worry.

Married or not, Walker Jacoby had a very sexy laugh.

The echo of his sexy laughter faded far too soon. Without it, the old inn was eerily quiet.

Hannah fought the urge to call him back. What would she say? That she had changed her mind? That this was all a big mistake?

Both were true.

However, neither fact changed a thing.

Hannah sank back into the chair, as the enormity of her situation hit her. What, oh what, had she gotten herself into?

She felt like falling to the floor and throwing a temper tantrum. Pounding the ground in frustration and railing to the gods. Screaming at the top of her lungs and demanding she get a do-over.

She had thrown a fit a time or two as a child, with mixed results. The ploy only worked with her mother, and only because Jacqueline Duncan hated making a scene.

Correction, Hannah thought with a grimace. Her mother hated anyone *else* making a scene, particularly if it stole attention away from her. The few times Hannah had pulled off a successful tantrum, she had been four years old and living in LA with her mother, where it was best to be seen, and not heard.

Two years and two attempts later, she discovered throwing a fit didn't work with her father. Terrell Duncan didn't mind hearing her scream and cry. He merely walked off and left her squirming in the floor of the Houston department store, staunchly refusing to buy her the toy she wanted.

With a sigh, Hannah knew throwing a fit hadn't worked then, and it wouldn't work now.

Her body felt a hundred years old as she dragged herself from the chair and forced herself to find the kitchen. If she was going shopping, she had to make a list.

The kitchen *looked* a hundred years old. It even had a full-sized, wood-burning, cast-iron stove against one wall. True, its modern-day counterpart stood across the room, but using the term 'modern' was generous. The monstrosity was woefully outdated, as was the original farmhouse sink and the commercial refrigerator. Hannah opened the double doors and peeked inside, just to make sure the thing still worked. A blast of cool air hit her in the face as she noted the shelves were completely bare.

There were a few canned goods in the pantry, canisters of sugar and flour, a generous supply of paper goods, and an unopened box of crackers. Other than that, there was no food left in the inn. Hannah made a note in her phone to buy *Everything.*

She started up the stairs to explore her sleeping quarters and what personal items she might need, but a new thought hit her. What if it took her longer than expected in town and it was dark by the time she returned? She couldn't fathom the idea of returning here in the dark, so she turned around, grabbed her purse, and started for the door. She made certain a light remained burning as she locked the door behind her and hurried to her car.

As she pulled away from the gate, she wondered what would happen if she simply kept driving and never looked back...

Fredericksburg looked like a delightful town, but there was no time to explore. By the time Hannah visited the western wear store and *Walmart*, the afternoon had quickly slipped away.

Driving back to the town that shared her name felt as if she were driving to her death. Dread welled low in her belly and rumbled in her chest like heartburn. A fine sheen of sweat broke across her brow. Could she do this? Was she strong enough? Brave enough?

She had little other choice. When *Lawrence, Schuster, and McMahon Investments* folded, so did her bank account. Her carefully planned career dried up faster than an alcohol wipe. No one wanted to hire David Lawrence's senior assistant; her close association to the firm left her tainted. And without a job, she could no longer afford her apartment. Without an apartment, she had nowhere to live.

She could have lived with JoeJoe, of course. He told her she was welcome to stay there, even while he was in Dubai for the month. She would be rattling around in the huge estate all by her lonesome, just her and the contractors he hired to gut and remodel the kitchen and all eight bathrooms. Come to think of it, he realized, staying there might not be such a good idea. Why didn't she go north, and check out her birthday present? What better, he asked gently, did she have to do?

Quite honestly, she had all but forgotten the ridiculous gift from four months prior. Her career as senior assistant at the firm kept her much too busy to even think of visiting the popular Texas Hill Country. A week's vacation was out of the question. The closest she came to taking time off was squeezing in a weekend bachelorette party in New Orleans. When she returned from the rushed trip, the world as she knew it came unraveled at the seams. Accused of embezzling funds from their clients, the firm where she worked fell under government control and all employees were immediately suspended, right along with their retirement accounts. Hannah had been fortunate to escape with her final paycheck and no investigation (at least, none that she knew of.)

With no job and no immediate prospects for future employment, she had ample time to wallow in self-pity. Making matters worse, with Jill's wedding, Hannah was officially the odd-woman-out; everyone else in her small group of friends was now married. That left her with no career, no man, and no friends with which to share her lonely Friday nights.

With her uncle headed to the Persian Gulf, her furniture headed to storage, and her friends well on their way to marital bliss, Hannah had headed north.

She blew out a blubbery sigh. Geographically, she may have traveled north, but she was headed south, all right. To a sentence of thirty days in Hannah, without bail.

Surely hell, or prison, couldn't be much worse.

CHAPTER 4

Hannah made her second trip from the car, arms filled with groceries and a case of water, when she spotted the biggest dog she had ever seen in her life. It looked more like a white, furry bear on all fours.

She stopped mid-stride, judging the distance between her and the building, versus her and the car. The inn was closer, but the white beast stood between her and the front door. No matter how big and bulky the animal appeared, she wasn't betting her life on being able to outrun it.

Willing herself to breathe deeply, she remembered Walker Jacoby's words, something about a wagging tail and adoring tongue. She saw neither of those now. She racked her brain, trying to recall the dog's name.

Just her luck, she had no trouble recalling the lawyer's sexy laugh, the one that erased all other thoughts from her head, but absolutely no recollection of the dog's name.

"Hi—Hi, there," she stammered. As an afterthought, she added a personable attempt, her voice wavering, "Doggie." *What was his name?* "Nice doggie, if only I could remember what to call you. No, no, don't come any closer. Is your name Fido? Duke? Benji?"

The beast stopped, turned its massive head to one side, and gave her a solemn gaze. Hannah saw a flash of teeth.

Her heart sank down to her toes. "Please tell me it's not Killer."

The dog dropped to its haunches and stared at her with dark, soulful eyes. Even sitting, the beast came as high as her waistline.

Hannah continued her guessing game. "Whitey? Bear?" She dared to take one step forward.

Bulk or not, the dog was quick to stand, instantly on alert.

"I really have to work on my listening skills," Hannah moaned, chiding herself aloud. She shifted the heavy case of water in her arms, daring another half step forward. "Oh, what did he tell me your name was? I think it was something common. Shaggy? Rover? Maybe it was Rock. No? Rocky, then?"

The dog's only response was to come a few steps closer.

"Wait. Wait. No need to come any closer, now is there, big boy? Max? You look like a Max. Oh, wait, that's it. It was a man's name... Jack? Buddy? Charlie? Let's try Barkley. Sam. Brutus." Her mind went blank on possible male names. "JoeJoe? Walker?"

The great white dog stopped and turned his head again, but this time he appeared to be looking just past her. He released a small whine, as if begging her to get it right this time.

From out of nowhere, the name came to her, as clearly as a whisper in her ear.

"That's it! Leroy!" she cried triumphantly.

The dog's ears twitched, and Hannah could have sworn his face lit up. His tail began a dance of pleasure.

"That's a good boy, Leroy," she purred. She bit her lip as the giant of a dog pranced its way forward. "Please be as friendly as the lawyer said you were."

The large white beast pushed against her, begging for attention, but the unexpected weight threw Hannah off balance. The case of water fell from her arms, barely missing the tip of the dog's wagging tail.

"Well, okay, guess my hand is free now," she muttered. She hesitantly reached out to touch his soft, furry head. "Good doggie. Good, *friendly*, doggie." Did psychology work with animals? "We're friends, right, Leroy? You're just sniffing me to get to know me, not to size me up for dinner. Right?"

The dog didn't answer. "Right, Leroy?" she pressed.

He opened his mouth, revealing long, needle-sharp cuspids. Hannah tried not to panic. She didn't know her dog breeds very well, but she thought he was some sort of sheep dog. She racked her brain for a useful snippet of information on the breed. *Sheep dogs are friendly, right? Gentle as a lamb, and all that.*

A long, pink tongue fell from the dog's mouth and wrapped around Hannah's hand, covering her in dog slobber. "Thanks, Leroy," she said dryly, trying not to flinch. Not when her hand was still so close to those cuspids and the hot, gaping hole that was his mouth. No need to insult him now, not when he was trying to establish a friendship. "Just what I wanted. Dog slime. Good doggie."

Hannah scratched the dog behind the ears and was rewarded with a look of adoration. Friendship firmly intact, she bent to retrieve her case of water and proceeded to the inn, the large white beast dancing around her legs.

"You're going to knock me down, you clumsy ox," she warned with a laugh, but he paid her no heed. When she reached the door, Leroy waited for her to enter first, and then pranced inside behind her.

"I'm not sure you belong in here, but at least you're a gentleman," she muttered.

As she worked to unload her groceries and stash them away, Hannah discovered that having the dog around made the huge, silent kitchen seem less empty. He watched her traverse back and forth across the space a dozen times before he grew bored and fell asleep.

When the great beast began to snore, the room was no longer silent.

"And here I was, thinking we could be roommates," Hannah clucked to the sleeping giant. "Not sure how much sleep I would get with you in the room."

Leroy's only response was a loud snort of unconcerned slumber.

By the time Hannah finished stashing away her purchases and changed outfits, she heard the rumble of a truck's engine. She told herself the stir in her blood was anticipation, not excitement. Walker Jacoby was married. This was merely a surge of relief, and the welcome anticipation of having another living soul on the property. A soul that didn't shed long white hair and snore like thunder.

She opened the front door, only to find herself pushed unceremoniously aside as Leroy lumbered his way through the opening. *So much for being a gentleman,* she sniffed. His large body wiggled and pranced in delight as he ran to greet their guest.

Hannah watched in resentment as Walker Jacoby laughed and reached down to stroke the white beast on his head. Why did the devil in blue jeans have to be so handsome? It was so much easier to despise an ugly man.

Parked as he was beneath a canopy of live oak branches, the sunlight filtered through the leaves and glistened in his dark hair, as it would off a raven's wing as it soared high across a cloudless Texas sky. Why couldn't the man have a nose like a bird's beak, Hannah groused, or little beady eyes set close together? He was hawking this ridiculous contract, after all, insisting they follow the letter of the law. Never mind that he was a lawyer and it was his job to enforce the terms of Wilhelmina Hannah's estate. He didn't have to *enjoy* it so much.

Listen to him now, she fumed silently, laughing as if he didn't have a care in the world. He probably didn't. He had unloaded this farce of a sale on her unsuspecting uncle and now *she* was the one left to pay the price. No wonder he sounded so jovial as he played with the furry giant, twirling him around in the dirt to tangle against his lithe, muscular thighs.

Not that she really noticed. She was looking more at the dog than she was the denim. Those denim-encased legs, she reminded herself, belonged to his wife, poor woman that she was. Now that Leroy had reared up on his hind legs and placed two dusty, giant paw prints practically on the man's shoulders, his wife would be taxed with washing away the evidence of their playful encounter. Good thing he had changed from his starched and monogrammed lawyer duds, she thought distractedly, into a t-shirt. The clinging white material was no longer so white as it stretched across his chiseled chest and sinewy arms.

Serves him right, Hannah sniffed, for wearing something that made him look even more masculine and attractive than he had earlier. But poor Mrs. Jacoby, who undoubtedly did the laundry for their household. He hardly looked the sort to pitch in with housework.

"Look what you did, doofus," Walker scolded the dog, affectionately pushing his hairy playmate away. He brushed at the dusty prints. "Now I'll have to pre-soak."

Reluctant to admit, even to herself, that she could be wrong about his helpfulness around the house, Hannah spoke from the doorway. Shading the filtered sunlight from her eyes, she called, "What breed is that monster, anyway?"

Noticing her presence for the first time, Walker nudged the dog away with his knee, preventing him from jumping again. "That's enough rough-housing for now," he instructed the beast. "Behave yourself. There's a lady present." He softened the rebuke by scratching the dog's massive head. "Leroy here," he informed Hannah, "is a registered Great Pyrenees. You come from a fine line of guardians, don't you, boy?"

"Guardian of sleep," Hannah muttered, allowing the door to shut behind her as she sauntered forward. "Have you heard that thing snore?"

Instead of answering, the lawyer assessed her change of clothes. "I see you found more suitable attire for our evening chores."

"I've heard that goats will eat just about anything. In an effort not to be one of those anythings, I wanted to look as unappetizing as possible." She indicated her jeans and simple t-shirt, but glanced up just in time to see the glimmer of contradiction in his blue eyes.

A married man ought not to look at another woman like that, she thought. *A married man ought not to find another woman so... appetizing.*

She might have told him so, had her tongue not been tied to the roof of her mouth.

An awkward moment hovered between them like a visible barrier. Leroy's sharp bark startled them both out of the moment, as he twirled on his heels and bounded toward Hannah. She deflected his exuberant greeting just in time, stretching her arms outward and laughing him away.

"Leroy."

The sharp ring in the lawyer's voice quieted the dog immediately. He dropped to his haunches and awaited further command. In a more amiable tone, Walker suggested, "Go feed Henny Penny."

Impressed, Hannah watched as the dog stood and dutifully trotted ahead to lead the way. "Henny Penny?" she asked, falling in step beside the lawyer.

"One of the laying hens."

Hannah surveyed the buildings clustered around the white-rocked road they traversed. They passed a weathered barn and set of corrals, situated closest to the inn. "The old livery stable, I presume?"

"Absolutely. This is where they kept fresh horses for the stage. Next to it was the blacksmith shop. You know, for making horseshoes, that sort of thing."

"And all those buildings across the way?"

"The far one on that side" —he indicated the structure closest to the gates— "is the old general store. You wouldn't believe some of the antiques still on the shelves. Next to it is the saloon, which later became a dance hall. Next to that was once another business. It had a variety of reincarnations and owners, including a dressmaker, a barber, and, there at the end, a small machine shop. It's probably in the worst shape of all the buildings, as you can see. The next two are cabins original to the town, and the last is the church."

She glimpsed the roof of another building through the trees. "And out there?"

"Another of the original cabins, now the home of Sadie and Fred."

Ahead of them, Leroy deviated from the road, instead taking a well-traveled path through the grass. They topped a small hill and Hannah saw the sheds and pens below, situated near the creek.

"And I guess that would be the farm," she murmured. She already heard the bleat of the goats and the unmistakable sound of a cow calling for its calf. Feet stalling, she balled up her fists and muttered beneath her breath, "JoeJoe is so dead."

"You said something?"

From the smirk on his face, the lawyer knew exactly what she said. He definitely understood the meaning behind the words, as well as the fervor in her tone.

"I asked, how many head?" she lied.

His blue eyes glittered with amusement. "Let's go see," he replied smoothly. He gallantly held out a hand. "After you."

Hannah marched down the hill, thankful she had changed into sensible athletic shoes. The muddy path would have ruined her expensive sandals.

"These are the goats," he pointed out needlessly.

Two small goats with brown spots and curly coats munched on a bale of hay in the corner of the pen, while a solid-dark goat nibbled on a piece of wire wrapped around a fence post. From the looks of it, it once held a rubber feed bucket. Only half a bucket remained, and it sported a jagged, gnawed-off edge. A white goat stood along the opposite fence, crying to something only it could see among the trees, calling out with its soulful, begging bleat. A black and white billy with small horns edged toward them, locked in a staring contest with Leroy. The two remaining goats in the pen scrambled to their feet and stood behind the billy in silent support.

"We keep the feed in this little shed. On the other side is the chicken coop."

Hannah gave him a suspicious eye. "You said 'we.' What, exactly, is it that you do here?"

When he shrugged his shoulders, she refused to notice how his tight shirt strained with the effort. The man should have the decency to wear another shirt over the snug-fitting tee, rather than flaunting his sculpted abs. *Why had his wife let him out of the house dressed like this?* She scowled to herself.

"I help out, here and there," Walker explained with a nonchalant air. He opened the feed barrel and peered inside. Apparently finding it empty, the man had the audacity to pluck a fifty-pound bag of feed from a nearby stack and lift it over his shoulder, as if it weighed no more than a bath towel. Muscles bulged and biceps flexed as he ripped open the seam and emptied the bag's contents into the barrel.

It was a noisy process, pouring the pellets into the metal container. He spoke over the din. "Sadie and Fred don't leave very often, but even when they're here, I stop in when I can. They aren't getting any younger, you know."

No, she didn't know. She didn't know a thing about the Tanner couple, or how to feed goats, or why her traitorous eyes followed his every move as he rolled up the empty sack, tied it with its own string, and stacked it neatly away for later disposal. For the life of her, she didn't know why she found this irritating, pompous, *married* man so maddeningly attractive.

"Now what?" she asked, her tone sharp with irritation aimed at herself.

"Now we feed the goats." He scooped an old coffee can into the barrel and filled it with pellets. Handing it to her, he showed Hannah where to pour the feed and told her how many cans were needed in each of the two troughs.

"The water trough should fill automatically, but sometimes the float gets stuck. If it does, you'll need to reach in and give it a little jiggle."

Hannah peered over his arm, to the slime-covered bottom he indicated. Bits of algae clung to the float and gave the water a faint greenish tint. "You expect me to put my hand in *there*?"

"I expect you to care for the goats and make certain they have plenty of water to drink each day," he countered in a firm voice. "The same can be said for the chickens."

Resisting the urge to crinkle her nose, Hannah moved forward. "You said the chickens were on this side? What keeps them... oh, I see. They have a fenced-in enclosure."

"More to keep prey out, than to keep them in," Walker explained. "Make sure you always latch this gate behind you."

He lifted the latch and stepped over the threshold, but Hannah's feet stalled. "I have to go *inside*? *With* them?"

A smirk played on his lips. "How else do you plan to collect the eggs?"

She crossed her arms over her chest and gave a curt reply. "I don't."

"You have to gather eggs every morning, Hannah. If you leave them too long, they'll spoil."

"But... But..." She knew she sputtered, even as she reluctantly followed him inside the pen.

"But what?"

"What if they attack me?"

Walker looked around at the docile birds, none of them giving the humans a second glance. Most scratched around in the dirt, two hunkered down to rest in the shade, and one fat, feathered fowl reigned supremely from a low perch atop an overturned bucket.

"Do these look like attack chickens?" he asked.

"Nnnooo," she agreed dubiously. "But you never can tell..."

"They won't hurt you. They may try to beat you to the feed bucket, but they won't hurt you."

He bent to retrieve the bucket from beneath the hen, shooing her away like a pesky fly. "Get off there, Goosey Loosey," he said. "How did you get this down to begin with?" Over his shoulder, he told Hannah, "It should hang here on this nail, so you can scoop it into the feed barrel. Just about a half bucket will do." He scooped it inside and came out with an offering of grains. "Here. Just scatter it around the yard."

"In the dirt?" she questioned.

"Yep, right there in the dirt. All around, not just in one spot."

When the chickens saw she had feed, they clucked noisily and scurried her way. With a squeal, Hannah dropped the bucket and took refuge behind the lawyer's back, tugging on his arm to shield her.

"What are you doing!" he cried in exasperation. "You spilled all the feed!"

"They're after me! They're going to attack me!"

He whirled around to glare at her, but she rotated with his every move, careful to keep him between her and the mob of hungry chickens. When he would have made a full circle and brought her in closer to the fowl, she quickly changed positions and scooted around in front of him, still clinging to his arm. The result found her pressed against his chest, his arm draped across her waist.

Walker looked down at her, his blue eyes dancing with wicked amusement. "If you wanted a hug," he drawled, "you could have just asked for it."

"I don't want a hug!" she snapped, even though she kept his arm tugged tightly around her. "I want protection!"

"From the girls?" His voice was incredulous. Stepping back, he freed his arm and used it to scoop up one of the chickens. "This vicious beast right here is Foxy Loxy. See how she has a pretty black and white pattern all over? She's a Dominicker. She'll lay a nice, big, brown egg for you." He thrust the large chicken toward her. "Here, pet her."

"I see how she has beady little eyes," Hannah murmured. She tentatively reached out to hover her hand over the chicken's head. The hen made a jerky movement, and Hannah snatched her hand away. "Did you see that? She tried to peck me!"

"She was just saying hello," Walker said, but he sat the hen down on the ground. She shook out her ruffled feathers and joined the scuffle around the spilled grain.

Using his booted foot to even out the heap of feed, Walker worked to distribute it better. Two of the chickens got into a feathered argument, squawking loudly at one another. Hannah watched from a safe distance.

Curiosity finally got the better of her. "So which one is Chicken Little?"

“That big rooster there, with all the red, green, and black feathers.”

“Isn’t that a misnomer?” Hannah asked with a bit of a smirk.

“I guess Miss Wilhelmina didn’t know how big he would get.” Satisfied with his work, Walker stepped back and allowed the chickens to scatter out the rest. Hands on his hips, he looked at the large, majestic rooster strutting their way. “Then again,” he considered, “maybe she did it on purpose. Miss Wilhelmina had a sense of humor about her.”

Hannah gave an unladylike snort. “She certainly did. This entire transaction is a joke!”

“I didn’t see your uncle laughing,” Walker reminded her, “when he paid for his purchase.”

“No, that’s because *I’m* the one paying the real price!”

Walker made no comment as he hung the bucket in its place and showed her where she would collect the eggs each morning. They stepped from the pen and he carefully latched the gate, giving it a little push for good measure.

“We’ll take the golf cart to check the cows,” he said, indicating the small utility vehicle she just noticed. “Hop in.”

As he slid behind the steering wheel, he returned to their previous conversation. “So, this purchase was a birthday present, huh?”

Hannah visibly cringed. “Yes. My uncle prides himself on giving... unique gifts. This is just one of a long list of doozies.”

At her tone, Walker Jacoby actually chuckled. “What were some of the others?”

"Well, let's see... instead of the pony I asked for on my seventh birthday, he gave me a retired Kentucky Derby race horse. When I was ten and wanted a magic kit, he took me to Vegas to meet a magician. I was terrified when they called me up on the stage to participate in a magic trick. I thought the man was truly sawing me in half." She laughed at the memory now, but at the time, it was traumatizing. "There was a full circus production in our backyard on my... fifth, I think it was, birthday... and a really cool private concert for me and five of my closest friends when I turned sixteen. And then there was the egg incident."

Walker sent her a sharp look, but the corners of his mouth lifted in amusement. "You say that with such drama. What, pray tell, was the egg incident?"

"For my twelfth birthday, JoeJoe gave me a dozen eggs, each in their own incubator. He claimed it was educational, but it turned into a science project that quite literally ate itself." The memory of it skittered over her skin, rippling her arms with gooseflesh. "In typical JoeJoe fashion, he had no idea what creatures would hatch forth out of those shells. Just my luck, I was living with my mother at the time, in a very swanky LA condo, where they had a strict no-crocodile/no-snake/no-duck policy."

She failed to mention that the fiasco offered her mother the perfect excuse to send young Hannah back to live with her father in Texas. Again.

The golf cart bounced over the rough terrain, but Walker never seemed to notice how Hannah hung on for dear life. "Well, fortunately for you, at least where the ducks are concerned, there are no such restrictions here in Hannah. You have a nice little gaggle of geese and ducks, right there in that pond."

She had to admit, if only to herself, it was a beautiful pond. Green banks sloped gently downward, tumbling gracefully into the crystal-blue shimmer. A half dozen or more ducks drifted on the tiny ripples of current, content to bask in the fading light of afternoon sun. Along the far banks, several geese waddled their way down the sloping grasses to plunk themselves, one by one, into the water. As the geese splashed into the pool, the water pushed away in ever-widening rings, until it reached the ducks in the middle of the pond. They bobbed up and down, riding on the waves of the ripple effect.

The scene exuded peace and calm. Hannah felt a bit of solitude slip into her soul.

Perhaps, just perhaps, this endeavor wouldn't be a colossal failure. Perhaps *she* wouldn't be a failure.

"There's fish in the pond, and even a nice little sandy bank over on the far left, if you're ever inclined to take a swim."

"I prefer swimming pools, thank you."

Walker just laughed, but for once, the sound wasn't condescending. "You're in the country now, Hannah. It may take a little getting used to, but once you let your guard down, I think you'll love it."

Hannah looked around her. It was beautiful, yes. The fields were awash with color, where Indian paintbrushes and vibrant bluebonnets weaved among the green grasses. Not to be outdone, the sun set low against the horizon, throwing out its last efforts of magnificence for the day. Strokes of pink and orange painted themselves against a backdrop of blue, swirling and dancing, blending into wisps of gilded white and brilliant gold. Unnamed colors streaked across the sky, creating a masterpiece that was already changing, already fading.

She would never say it aloud, not to this man, but she seldom saw a sky like this in Houston. It could have been the skyscrapers that stood between her and nature's glorious paintings. Or it could have been her career.

Either way, this was a treat to behold. Even the air felt different here. It felt lighter. More natural. It certainly smelled differently. Clean and fresh. *Real.* Hannah closed her eyes and inhaled a deep breath, enjoying the silence around her, imagining that she didn't have a care in the world.

The nearby lowing of a cow jarred her from her dream world, reminding Hannah that her life wasn't quite so carefree. An audible sigh escaped as she pulled herself back to reality. She may as well get it over with now, and hear the worst of it. "Tell me about this milk cow I own."

CHAPTER 5

By the time they returned to the inn, twilight had fallen. Lit with electric lanterns along the front of the building, the old whitewashed limestone and lumber structure fairly glowed against the darkening sky, taking on an ethereal feel. Just for a moment, Hannah imagined she was stepping through a portal of time. Stepping up to the ancient dwelling was like stepping back into the past.

"Were there ever any Old West outlaws around here?" she asked suddenly.

The lawyer gave her a sharp look. "Why would you ask a thing like that?"

Once the words were out, she felt foolish having spoken them. She gave a lame shrug of her shoulders. "I don't know. Something about it just feels so... western. Like it's straight out of a movie. Was the stage coach ever robbed en route to here?"

His answering shrug was dismissive. "Times were rough back then." He motioned toward her car. "Do you need a hand with your luggage, or have you already unloaded?"

In truth, she hadn't given a thought to her luggage, perhaps because she was avoiding the thought of spending the night here. "Not yet," she said.

"Need help?"

"Sure." It was more that she wasn't ready to be left alone yet, than actually needing his help.

"Which room will be yours?"

"I haven't gone further than the kitchen," she admitted.

"If you'll unlock the car, I'll bring everything in," he offered. "Why don't you go on in and choose a room?"

"Any room?"

He gave her a charming smile. "They all belong to you now. You can have your pick."

With a smile like that, Hannah didn't want him anywhere near while she selected a bed. She hastily gave him the code to her car's keypad. While he headed to the car, she hurried inside the inn and up the stairs. She invited Leroy to come with her.

The dog trotted ahead of her to lead the way, his sharp claws clicking against the wooden steps. Hannah wondered how many feet had taken this very path over the years, up the steep staircase to the rented rooms.

The stairs led to a long corridor that stretched in either direction, bisecting the second floor in half. If not for the whitewashed walls and the electric lanterns at regular intervals, the hallway would have been dark and gloomy. No windows beckoned from either corridor to offer the promise of sunshine. Instead, Hannah saw exposed brick on either endcap.

There weren't many bedrooms in the old inn. Seven, to be exact. The largest was in the left front corner, with windows overlooking the town's entrance and the front driveway. Given the room's strategic location—she would see trouble the moment it rolled through the gates—this would be hers.

"Hannah?" She heard Walker's voice as he started up the stairs.

"In the corner room!" she called.

"There's four corners," he called back.

She stuck her head out the door and saw him top the stairs, arms loaded with all her luggage. He made the effort look easy, even though she knew that her large suitcase weighed just slightly less than a full-grown elephant. Not knowing how long she would be gone and what she would be dressing for, she did the logical thing and brought most of her wardrobe with her.

"Good choice," he said, nodding his approval. "That's the master suite."

She knew a moment of uncertainty. "Wait. The former owner didn't die here, did she?"

"Why? Afraid of ghosts?" He pushed past her, giving the first hint that his load might be heavy. She got a whiff of his cologne, mingled with the twang of manly sweat. Together, it was a dangerous combination.

"A little," she admitted. She jutted her chin out, challenging him to make something of it. Namely, that there were no such things as ghosts.

"To my knowledge, all ghosts around these parts are friendly," he assured her, depositing the suitcases to the floor. He looked around for a flat surface, saw what he wanted, and hefted the heaviest suitcase onto the top of a long, low chest of drawers. "Hope the legs hold on this thing," he said. "Don't know why you felt the need to bring a ton of bricks with you, but here you go. And in answer to your question, Miss Wilhelmina didn't die in this room."

"Good. And for my own piece of mind, I won't ask for further details. Just in case she died in a different room here at the inn," she clarified.

Hannah steadfastly ignored the implications of his answering smirk.

"Oh, that blue duffel bag isn't mine."

"I know. It's mine."

"Why do you need a duffel bag?" She eyed it suspiciously. "Don't tell me it's full of more papers I have to sign!"

"No, those are in my briefcase, and there are just two," he assured her. He nodded toward the bag in question. "Those are my clothes," he explained.

"Why do you need clothes?"

"I know you are uncomfortable with the idea of staying here alone, at least for the first few nights. I consulted the terms of the contract, and even though you aren't allowed to leave the property, there's nothing that says you can't have company. I thought I'd stay a couple of nights, until you get settled in and feel at home."

"You're going to stay *here*?" She indicated the floor at her feet.

"Well, not in *your* room, I'm not."

Her face flamed, particularly seeing the glimmer of amusement in his blue eyes. "Of course, not in my room!" she snapped.

Noting the look of consternation upon her face, he frowned. "Look, I thought I was doing you a favor. If you'd rather I not stay..."

Hannah opened her mouth to say something, but promptly shut it. *Did* she want him to stay?

On the one hand, the thought of staying here alone in the house was terrifying.

On the other hand, the thought of being alone in the house, *with* him, struck an entirely different kind of terror within her thundering heart.

Her mouth flapped open and shut, like a dying fish, sucking in its last few gulps of life.

"I'll need an answer before midnight," he taunted.

"Fine." Her tone was brusque. "Pick a room."

Walker arched his eyebrow in silent reprimand. They both knew it was a rude acceptance to a very gallant offer. Without another word, he bent to retrieve his bag and strode from the room, Leroy close on his heels.

Shaking off the affront, Hannah sniffed her indifference and moved the rest of her luggage from the middle of the floor. She didn't bother unpacking just yet.

Until she signed the final two papers, she still had time to change her mind and back out of this whole ridiculous deal...

Hunger drove her back downstairs. Hannah realized she hadn't eaten since her drive down this morning. Despite the ever-growing knot in her stomach, she suddenly felt weak from hunger.

She hadn't planned on meals for two. She tried to bite back the stab of resentment, knowing, as she did, she couldn't return to town for an entire month.

"I can pick up more groceries in town tomorrow," Walker said from behind her.

She hadn't heard him come in. She gave a squeal of surprise and promptly banged her hand on the shelf as she whirled around.

"Don't you know how to shuffle those boots you wear," she snapped crossly, "instead of sneaking up on a soul like that?"

"I didn't know I was sneaking."

"You were. You did. And look what happened." She held up her hand as proof of his nefarious deed.

He pursed his lips, unsure of what he was seeing. "You have graceful hands?" he guessed. "A broken fingernail?"

"Where?" She jerked her hand down to examine her perfectly manicured nails. All ten were intact. "I don't have a broken nail." A new thought occurred to her. "How am I supposed to keep it that way, if I can't leave the compound?"

"It's not a compound, Hannah. It's a *town*." He enunciated the word for emphasis.

"So you say."

He overlooked her cross reply. "I thought I'd help you cook," he offered. "If you'd like, I can grill something on the barbecue pit."

"I put all the meat in the freezer. I was planning on a baked potato, stuffed with broccoli and cheese."

"That's fine. I can stop at the meat market tomorrow. What do you prefer—steak, fish, or chicken?"

Her grouchy attitude gave way and she ventured a saucy smile. "I have to choose?"

"Not really. I'll get all three." His own smile was disarming. "And if you like sausage, this is the German sausage capitol of Texas, you know."

"By all means, bring sausage, too."

"I know just the place to go. In fact, I'll bring the whole meal," he decided. "Matousek's Market makes the best sausage and the best schnitzel you've ever tasted. We can always cook the next night."

There was something unsettling about the thought of sharing her evening meals with this man. Reaching for the potatoes, she kept her voice casual as she started scrubbing two large spuds. "Do I need a third potato? Will Mrs. Jacoby be joining us for supper tonight?"

He gave her an odd look, his brow furrowed with confusion. "No," he said slowly, as if the thought was absurd.

He had such an odd reaction, Hannah couldn't help but push for more information. "She doesn't mind you staying here?"

Walker turned away to search for plates among the overhead cabinets. "She didn't say anything, so I guess not," he said over his shoulder.

Maybe they're separated, Hannah considered. Staying here with her wouldn't help any, if they were having marriage problems. Yet for the life of her, she didn't have the gumption to insist he go home to his wife. It had nothing to do with the pull of attraction she felt toward him. It had everything to do with the fact she was scared to death to stay in this rambling old inn, all by herself.

She felt a pang of sympathy toward the man. She hated to see any marriage falter and fail, even when the husband was a cad like Walker Jacoby.

It wasn't an entirely accurate account, she knew. However, it was far safer to think of him in uncharitable terms, rather than to admit the attorney might actually be an all right sort of guy. He didn't have to stay with her. And he didn't have to bring meals, even if he was sharing them with her. It surprised her that he was stepping in and offering to help in the kitchen.

She hadn't given him enough credit, she realized.

"Do you want to eat here in the kitchen, or out in the dining room?" he asked, holding the makings for two place settings in his hands.

The kitchen seemed too intimate, so she motioned toward the large room out front. "I think the dining room, don't you?"

"Fine by me."

Hannah popped the potatoes in the microwave and prepped the broccoli. In less than twenty minutes, the simple meal was ready.

Again, Walker Jacoby surprised her. He bowed his head and said grace, asking for Hannah's success in her new endeavor. After the amens, she sent him a questioning look, but he simply winked and said, "Mrs. Jacoby would never forgive me if I didn't ask a blessing before every meal."

Bless her heart, his wife is a Christian woman, Hannah mused. *Even more reason for me to remember: HE'S MARRIED.*

She screamed the reminder to herself.

They talked about the animals while they ate. Hannah asked numerous questions, surprising herself that she was actually curious. Walker told her he would help gather eggs and milk the cow the following morning, before he left for the office.

They said goodnight in the kitchen, after Walker assured her he would do the dishes and lock up for the night.

"Leroy?" she questioned, before heading to the stairs. The hairy beast dozed in the corner, where he had been all through the meal.

"Is a watch dog. He sleeps during the day, prowls at night. I'll put him out before I close up."

So much for having a roommate, she mused.

It was still early, at least by her normal schedule. Hannah vaguely remembered some old adage about early to bed, early to rise. Something else about farmers getting up at the crack of dawn. She wasn't sure any of it applied to her, but she knew she was exhausted.

If there was ever a day when she needed a glass of wine, this was it. Good thing she brought a bottle upstairs. After unpacking the bare minimum for the night, Hannah slipped into a pair of pajama pants and a camisole top, carried her bottle of wine outside to the balcony, and poured herself a full goblet.

The air was clean and clear, the night pleasantly warm. High above her, a plane arced in a silent path across the dark sky. The sounds of night were all around her. Frogs croaking,

crickets chirping, a lonely owl calling for its mate. A car traveling down the highway, although the sound was singular. So
unlike the city, she mused, where it was difficult to hear anything above the relentless roar of traffic. Even in the dead of
night, the city never slept.

She sipped on her wine, welcoming the slack that crawled
into her muscles. The knots slowly came untied, the tension
finally unbuckled. She lay her head onto the curve of the
chair's back, forcing her mind into a blank slate. Willing herself not to think, not to worry. Not to panic.

Tomorrow, she would curse her uncle's foolish extrava-
gance. Her father always did say his little brother had more
money than he had good sense. For once, she was apt to agree.
Tomorrow, she would call JoeJoe in Dubai and give him a
piece of her mind. She would throw her fit, for all the good it
would do her.

Tomorrow, she would panic. By this time tomorrow night,
she would be a farmer. She would have gathered her first eggs
and—gulp—milked her first cow. Tomorrow, she would have
the stain of the country life upon her hands.

Tomorrow, she would explore her new world. Cut ties with
her old one. She would cancel upcoming appointments, and
make plans of a different sort, here in her new world. Tomorrow, she would unpack her suitcase and, for better or for
worse, she would settle in.

But that was all tomorrow.

Tomorrow would come soon enough.

Tonight, she would sit here in the night air, content to hear
the sounds of her new surroundings cocoon her within its wel-

coming web. Maybe it was the wine, maybe it was the stars. Stars she could actually see, without the glare of neon lights and buildings that climbed their brightly illuminated way into the sky. Something about the peace and quiet called to her, soothed her in a way she had never known. Relaxed her.

Before she finished her first glass of wine, the soft bleat of the goats reached her ears. She couldn't bring herself to care. The cows joined in by the time she poured her second glass. Oddly enough, she found the sounds comforting. A mother and her calf, calling to one another in the darkness.

And when the fiddle music started, she sipped slowly on her wine and lost herself to the soft, mournful notes floating on the breeze. The sweet melody wrapped around her and coaxed the last of the coils from her body.

Walker Jacoby was just full of surprises. A smart, handsome lawyer who did the dishes, babysat frightened clients, and played the fiddle.

Maybe, she mused, emptying her wine glass and closing her eyes in contentment, *Mrs. Jacoby isn't so unfortunate, after all.*

Maybe she was one lucky woman.

CHAPTER 6

Morning came early. The moonlight and the melody gave way to the light of day and, although not exactly the break of dawn, it was suddenly tomorrow. The harsh reality of her new life began.

"You want me to put my hand *where*?"

Hannah stared at the lawyer, hands propped defiantly upon her hips. She stood in a wide-legged, dig-in-your-heels stance. If it were truly the Old West, she would be drawing her six guns about now.

"On her teats, like this," he said evenly. "You have to grab them and pull."

"Have you lost your mind!" It wasn't a question.

"No, Hannah, I haven't. How else did you think you were going to milk a cow?"

Her eyes were frantic. Her hands came off her hips to gesture wildly. "I don't know. I thought maybe there was a machine or something. That maybe it just sort of... gushed out. I didn't think I would have to—to *touch* her!"

Some of his cool was slipping. A heated impatience edged into his voice. "I can't stay here all morning. I have appointments. Either I help you do this now, or you do it on your own, after I leave. Your choice."

She took a hesitant step forward.

"Come on, you survived gathering the eggs," he reminded her.

"Just barely! Henny Penny almost took my hand off!"

"She gave you a little peck. There's not even a mark."

"Cocky Locky chased me out of the pen."

"She thought you had feed in the bucket. I told you to bring a basket from the house." He motioned her forward. "You can do this, Hannah. It's really not hard, once you get the hang of it."

When she was within snagging distance, he grabbed her hands and rubbed them briskly between his own.

"What are you doing?" she cried, trying to pull away.

"Your hands are like ice."

"Fear always does that to them."

"That's why I'm warming them up. How would you like cold hands on your... on you?"

She refused to think about his hands, cold or otherwise, on her corresponding body parts.

She tossed her head, her dark ponytail swinging. "I'm still not touching that cow."

His tone brooked no argument. "Yes. You are."

It was difficult to maintain eye contact with the man. "I guess you use that steely-eyed glare on the jury, swaying them to do your bidding." Her tone was accusing. "But it won't work with me," she claimed.

Eyes locked on hers, hands clasped around her wrists, he stepped backwards, pulling her with him. Before she knew it, she bent down in tandem with him, and he pressed her fingers around two dangling appendages. They were smooth and swollen, like the fingers of a water-filled glove. The strength of both their hands—his fingers pressing into hers, forcing her to make a grip—massaged the plump vessels. Walker jerked her hands downward, then up again. Soon, he had a rhythm going. One hand went up, the other down. And finally, the reward came. The ping of milk, hitting the empty bottom of the pail.

Hannah forgot to be angry. She forgot that she was doing this under duress. That she said she would *never* milk a cow. In the excitement of the moment, she forgot to sulk.

"I'm doing it!" she cried, her face alight with accomplishment. She turned to make certain Walker witnessed her victory, and found his face disturbingly close. Her hands faltered.

"Don't stop now," he urged, his smile wide. "We're just getting started."

"But..."

"Stay with me, Hannah. Right hand, tug. Left hand, tug. Right hand, tug. That's it, tug. You got it, tug."

Hannah stayed with it until Buttercrunch turned to look at her. The proximity of those large brown eyes and the moist, black nose frightened her. When the cow gave a gentle moo and slurped her long tongue out, Hannah jerked away, almost upsetting the milk bucket in the process.

"I'll finish up here, if you'll make friends with Buttercrunch," Walker bargained with her.

"Fr—Friends?"

"Yeah, you know. Stroke her head. Pat her neck. Make friends."

"You're enjoying my humiliation, much too much," she muttered beneath her breath. She put a tentative hand out to touch the cow's head. One ear twitched in response, but the cow allowed the attention. "What's with the names? You called one Vanilla Bean last night."

"They're named after Blue Bell flavors. It's the unofficial ice cream of Texas, and Sadie and Fred's personal favorite. They named most of the herd."

"Who named the chickens?"

"Miss Wilhelmina."

"After a children's fairy tale."

He shrugged and continued to fill the bucket, one squirt at a time.

❦

Fresh milk had a distinct taste, one that Hannah wasn't sure she liked. She expected the milk to be thick and creamy, not thin and weak tasting. Walker assured her it was an acquired taste, but she wasn't convinced.

With the animals tended to, Walker left for work. The old inn seemed quiet without his presence there, but Hannah was determined to have a productive day.

Right after she called her uncle.

It was nine hours later in Dubai than it was here in Texas. *Good*, she thought with malicious glee. *I'll spoil his supper.*

Her uncle, however, wasn't answering her calls. She left three heated messages, before giving up and moving on to the next task on her to-do list. A handful more calls, most as voice messages, and she set her phone aside. Time to tackle her suitcases.

It took longer than she anticipated, unpacking and finding proper places for all her things. It was more complicated than merely finding a temporary spot to store her clothes. She would be here for an unspecified amount of time. Months, most likely, or at least until JoeJoe's lawyers could find a loophole in which she could work her way through. She could always move her things to her liking later on, but why do double work?

The master suite was large and roomy, with ample storage and little excess furniture. The headboard looked antique, although Hannah wondered when the queen-size mattress was invented. At any rate, the carvings were unique and hand-tooled, making it a stunning piece in pale wood. By contrast, the low chest of drawers—the one with the sturdy legs, strong enough not to bow beneath her suitcase—was made of dark mahogany, and polished to a low sheen. The other pieces were all antique and ranged in color and style, making for an informal but eclectic mix.

Hannah's favorite was a painted chest with three drawers of staggered sizes. The piece was very old, with original pale green milk paint. Although faded with time, a painted trail of green ivy snaked along the bones of the chest, intermingling with tiny images in a rainbow of colors, now bleached with age. She fingered the different emblems, even as she wondered from where their inspiration came. A crooked tree, an ear of corn, and a flower. Was that a cloud, or a body of water? That checkered item was more likely a fence, than a railroad. Certainly not a hashtag, not back then. She made out a brown triangle, and a tiny, once-red barn. Something else looked like a flock of black birds. The artist had a distinct talent, even though the subject matter was odd and varied. Still, it was an interesting piece.

Typical of old houses, there was no closet. A massive oak wardrobe occupied one full wall in the bathroom, but Hannah rather liked the convenience. At least the master bath had been updated sometime within the last decade.

A sitting room completed the suite. The couch was small and old, but there was a graceful side chair that, upon closer inspection, proved to be a recliner. Positioned across from a flat-screen television set, Hannah imagined it was Miss Wilhelmina's favored spot in the house.

The writing desk would be just right for her laptop, Hannah decided. She visualized her own books in the nearby bookcase, not the odd collection of titles now in place.

The books were one of the few reminders of the past owner. Most of Wilhelmina Hannah's personal effects were long since removed from the rooms. Hannah saw less-faded patches upon the walls, evidence of frames that once resided there. The only pictures on the papered walls now were scenes of bucolic pastures, ripe with Texas bluebonnets and the wild-flowers of spring.

Satisfied that most of her possessions now had a home, Hannah stashed the empty suitcases in a corner and went down in search of something to eat. A quick salad fueled her for some afternoon exploration.

Taking the ring of keys Walker had given her, and with Leroy by her side, Hannah set out across the dusty driveway. The old general store was her first stop.

Just as the attorney told her, the walls and top shelves were lined with relics from the past. Some were behind glass; others were exposed to the thick element of dust in the old building. Hannah recognized some of the items as true antiques: a glass butter churn and its wooden predecessor, a two-man hand saw, a variety of tin pails, scoops, cans, and utilitarian gadgets, old tools, and an early radio. Many of the items were passed-over wares, left sitting on the shelf because no one had purchased them. Again, Hannah recognized several of the brands as defunct. This may very well be the last place on Earth still shelving the items.

Surely, she thought, this was more for show than for sale. After a moment's study, she understood the pattern. Everything on the top, hard-to-reach shelves was merely for show. The items on the lower shelves, eye level and below, were for sale. While more current, their offerings were sparse and erratic. Small toys and tourist-trap trinkets shared shelf space with hard candy and rolls of paper towels. Hannah was surprised to see a small offering of canned goods and cases of water; she was even more surprised to see they all were within the expiration date.

Who buys this stuff? Surely, few motorists stopped in to shop.

The glass front, reach-in cooler was empty, leaving Hannah to wonder what usually filled the shelves. She could hardly see milk and vegetables staying fresh, not without someone to buy and consume them. And what was that ancient old scale used for? Decades before digital, the dials spun and numbers rolled as she put her finger on the smooth surface and gently pressed down.

Resurrecting rusty math skills, Hannah did the quick calculations in her head. One and four tenths of an ounce, for the cost of about a quarter.

Pfft. Surely, I'm worth more than that. She looked around, her mouth curling into a self-deprecating sneer. *After all, I own a **town** now. Woo hoo.*

The checkout counter looked almost serviceable. Neat stacks of brown paper bags, in a range of sizes. A handheld calculator and, of all things, a credit card machine. With chip compatibility, no less, so it had to be current. Postcards touting the images of the iconic Hill Country, and a small selection of handcrafted notecards. Even a half-filled box of those spinning gadgets, and a handful of selfie sticks. Both seemed strangely out of place next to the antique cash register.

The register was an intricate piece, fashioned of shiny metal and decorative scrolling. Tall and heavy, with round buttons like she had seen on the very first typewriters. Hannah depressed one button at random, just to see if it still worked.

With a distinctive *cha-ching* and the clatter of metal against metal, the heavy cash drawer popped out with unexpected force. It caught Hannah in the wrist and made her howl.

"Holy boomtown!" she cried, using a phrase her oilman uncle had coined. "There's still money in there!" She didn't dare touch it, but she saw a decent amount of start-up cash in the till.

"Obviously," she said aloud to no one but herself, "this store is more operational than I thought. I guess it hasn't been out of business for very long."

She left the store exactly as she found it, turning out the lights and locking the door. As she made her way to the next building, she wondered if Miss Wilhelmina had worked the store until her death. That would explain the current merchandise.

The saloon and dance hall could have been from any old movie set. Old advertising signs, hand-painted in bright colors and vintage fonts, lined the stark wooden walls. It was hard to imagine a time when telephone calls were placed using a mere five digits, but the proof was here. 'Dial JH-479' and 'Call Hal, MK-261' beckoned from overhead. The sheer simplicity of some of the advertisements, 'Try it! It's good!', made Hannah smile.

Ancient Wanted Posters, most of them appearing authentic rather than reproduced, graced the walls of the old saloon. Some were ragged, some were under glass. All were faded and ominous. What had these men done, Hannah wondered, to warrant a price on their heads? More than one was wanted *Dead or Alive*, his fate at the hands of a bounty hunter, professional or not. She shivered as she studied one faded and grizzly face, an evil-looking man with a patch over his eye and a deep scar on his cheek. Maurice 'Patch' Hatfield, wanted dead or alive, for robbing a stagecoach and killing its driver.

"He must have been someone famous," she guessed aloud, "seeing as his poster warranted a glass frame. Glad I'll never meet up with him." Just looking at his scarred face sent shivers up her spine, and Hannah swore she felt a chill swirling the air around her.

Shaking off the sensation, she wandered further down the walls, covered here with old advertising posters. A rodeo from 1951, featuring the popular Hank Williams. A county fair a few years later, introducing a newcomer named Elvis Presley. And here on this very stage in Hannah, Texas, 1963, a dance featuring neighbor Willie Nelson.

With new appreciation, Hannah wondered up to the bandstand, situated across the yawning space from the long bar. Her mind spun fantasies of who had stood here in the past, and of who might grace the stage in the future. This would make an awesome venue for a wedding reception. A huge, open floor plan. Room for a band. Ample space for a dance floor, plus tables. A working bar. She saw spigots for tap beer, room for under-counter coolers, and an array of glassware. With a few strings of white lights and a bit of imagination, the space could easily transform into rustic chic.

The building adjacent to the saloon was in worse condition than she had imagined, but the two cabins were a pleasant surprise. The smaller of the two had been carefully and lovingly restored, boasting modern day conveniences in rustic disguise.

A weathered panel slid aside to reveal a flat-screen television. An upside down pail in the tile-lined shower housed a multi-jet showerhead. Rippled tin and age-grooved wood were charming backdrops for everything a guest might need during a weekend stay. Just one bedroom, but with a pullout sofa to accommodate more.

The other cabin had two bedrooms and a wonderful old claw-foot tub. While similarly furnished and comfortable looking enough, it lacked the detail of its smaller counterpart. It struck Hannah as more dated, less darling. However, with a few embellishments and some well-orchestrated adjustments, she knew it had the same potential as the first cabin.

The old church was simple and elegant. Perfect, Hannah thought, for a wedding.

Her mind whirled with possibilities as she and Leroy walked back to the inn. Did she dare put voice to the thoughts in her head? Did she acknowledge this crazy notion that already took shape in her imagination?

Could Hannah, Texas really become a wedding venue? It had the basic elements for success...

A place for the ceremony. Two, in fact, if the couple preferred an outdoor wedding by the pond.

A place for the reception. Plenty of room for dancing and dining.

Rooms for the wedding party and out-of-town guests. Two private cabins, plus six rooms at the inn. She didn't remember all the room details—didn't one have two double beds, another have a couch? Off the top of her head, Hannah counted accommodations for at least twenty or more guests.

I know nothing about running an inn, much less a wedding venue, Hannah chided herself. *I must be insane. Maybe I had too much wine last night. Too much fresh air and sunshine this morning. Inhaled chicken fumes, or cow gas. Something strong enough to knock my good sense loose. I can't honestly be thinking what I'm thinking!*

Can I?

Intent on questioning her own sanity, Hannah didn't see the woman at first. A faint noise drew her attention, the sound of a breeze stirring among the loose edges of paper. To her surprise, a young woman stood at the front desk, fingering the guest ledger, a book Hannah had yet to examine.

"May I help you?" Hannah asked, trying not to sound as unsettled as she felt. Where was the woman's car? Moreover, why was she dressed so oddly? She wore a lovely yellow dress, sprigged with little white flowers and featuring a very full circular skirt, but it was hardly something one wore every day. It was best suited for a costume ball, particularly if one were going as a Southern belle from a century long past.

The woman looked every bit as surprised as Hannah felt. "Oh, goodness me. I didn't know anyone was here." She spoke with a heavy Southern accent, honeyed and drawled with just the right amount of charm.

"Yes, I'm the—" she faltered, unsure of how to identify herself. She didn't feel like an innkeeper, no matter what the legal papers said. Saying she was staff sounded too impersonal. She finally went with a simple, "I'm Hannah. May I help you?"

The young woman had the grace to flush. A soft rosy glow appeared on cheeks as pale and pure as the milk in this morning's bucket. *She needs to get more sun*, Hannah thought absent-ly. *At least a darker shade of base. She's as pale as a ghost!*

"I'm sorry," the woman purred. Everything about her was pale, in an exquisite, feminine sort of way. Her golden hair was curled into perfect ringlets, almost a perfect color match to her long yellow dress. Her eyes were light blue, her skin almost translucent. Her voice was as soft and dainty as her appearance. "I wasn't aware someone would see me."

Hannah was rudely reminded of her own attire. Blue jeans, t-shirt with a smear of cow slobber, new but already scuffed cowboy boots, and a ponytail from early this morning. Hardly the kind of thing she normally wore, and now a sad comparison to this beautiful woman, odd dress and all.

"I fear I was peeking at your guest ledger," she admitted. "I'm searching for my beau. I was hoping he had been here."

Recognizing the tactic as highly unconventional and reeking of privacy invasion, Hannah reached out to slide the ledger from the woman's reach. Her petite fingers hovered just over the book, not quite touching it, but Hannah saw no need in offering further opportunity. She slipped behind the counter and pretended to thumb through the book in an offer of help.

"Is this Bo your husband?" she asked.

The woman gave her a strange look. Hannah thought she may have frowned, but the lighting was dimmer than she realized. She suddenly had trouble making out the blonde's features, even at such short range. Hannah made a mental note to install brighter bulbs.

"No," the woman finally said. "He's my intended."

It was an odd way of describing her fiancé. Hannah glanced at her ringless finger and wondered if the claim were true. No matter, there were still privacy laws prohibiting her from sharing such information.

At least, Hannah assumed there were. She would need to brush up on hospitality rules and regulations.

Listen to me, acting as if I'm truly considering this farce of an arrangement!

"Have you seen him?" the blonde asked, the tremble of worry slipping into her voice.

"I'm sorry, but I'm new here. I just arrived yesterday."

"If you see him, please be so kind as to tell him that Caroline is looking for him. I'll not give up, not until I see my love again!" She spoke with soft fervor as she put a lacy handkerchief to her nose and sniffed.

The action would have been outrageously dramatic, had it not been so sincere. With a stab of sympathy, Hannah thought she understood. Perhaps the poor woman had lost her lover to a tragic death, and her mind couldn't accept reality. Perhaps she had always been this way, or perhaps the loss had pushed her over the edge. Either would explain the odd attire and the general air of mystique shrouding her.

"Yes, certainly," Hannah agreed with a pitied smile.

"Bless your heart," Caroline replied, her own smile serene.

Leroy barked, looking toward the front windows. He ran up and down the long room, his sharp bark piercing as it rose and echoed in the tall spaces.

"Leroy, quiet," Hannah instructed, trying to interject the same sense of authority she had heard in Walker's command yesterday.

When the dog continued to bark, clearly on alert, Hannah excused herself and rounded the counter to see what caused the commotion. Peering out the windows, she saw vague movement in the trees, but it could have easily been the wind. A rabbit, even, or a bird.

"I'm sorry about that," she murmured, turning back to address her guest.

Caroline was nowhere to be seen. Only a faint trace of her perfume remained, a light hint of lavender lingering in the air. With a frown, Hannah called the woman's name. She peeked into the kitchen, and the small powder room off the hall. There was no sign of her. Certain she wasn't downstairs, Hannah took the staircase up. Clearly, Caroline had decided to search the rooms for herself. For the first time, Hannah considered the fact the woman might be dangerous. She faltered on the steps, but knew it was unacceptable for an unauthorized visitor to go nosing through the rooms. Good thing the rooms were all empty. The woman had no business being upstairs.

"Caroline?" Hannah called from the landing. "I'm afraid I must insist..."

Her voice trailed off as she watched the woman exit the room at the far end of the hall. She never heard the door close. In fact, she could have sworn the door was securely fastened and never moved. But that was impossible. One moment the hallway was empty, and the next moment Caroline was there, in her long yellow dress and its wide circular skirt. A hoop skirt, she thought it was called, just like the Southern belles of the Old South once wore.

A sense of unease came over Hannah. A chill worked its way down her spine and manifested itself as gooseflesh.

"C—Caroline?" she managed to croak.

From down the long corridor, the blond woman looked forlorn. "He's not there," she reported in a sorrowful voice. "My love has vanished."

"How did you—" Before she could finish her sentence, Caroline turned and disappeared.

Hannah frowned. She didn't remember another hallway, but obviously, she had missed it. Curiosity pushed her forward. Maybe she was unaware of a back stairwell.

But when Hannah reached the end of the hall, there was no exit. Just as she remembered, she quite literally hit a brick wall. She now knew it was part of the massive chimneys bracketing either side of the inn, an early precursor to central heating. Where had Caroline gone? How did she vanish into thin air? There weren't any windows, and the door to Room 5 was locked. Hannah checked.

From the great room below, Leroy barked again, and this time, he was more agitated than before. Torn between looking for Caroline and seeing what upset the white beast below, Hannah wavered with uncertainty. When Leroy began to growl, she made her decision. She hurried down the stairs, just in time to see a flash of color pass by the front window.

However she had done it, Caroline had managed to get downstairs and out of sight, all before Hannah could reach the door.

CHAPTER 7

The motel door banged against the wall, announcing his brother's arrival. It startled the man in front of the television set, breaking his concentration. He had mentally tallied up the value of the last showcase, and Drew Carey was about to reveal the price. He'd missed the first one by almost twenty thousand dollars, but this guess was right on the money. He could feel it.

One eye on the television set, one eye on his brother, he asked, "How'd it go? What'd you see?"

The big man threw his hat on the motel bed in disgust. "Not a dad burned thing. There was a huge white dog, big as a polar bear, raising a ruckus that could wake the dead. Couldn't get close enough to see a thing, don't you know."

"Shoulda shot the darn thing," his brother advised. "There ain't no bear season round here, is there?"

"It wasn't a bear, you idiot, it was just big as one!"

"I get awful tired of you calling me an idiot, big brother."

"Well, I get awful tired of you *acting* like one!" he shot back. "I couldn't shoot the dog. He was inside the house."

"What house?"

"The old hotel, you nitwit. Pay attention. And turn off that dad-blamed TV!"

With a disgruntled snort, his brother complied. "Missed it by fifteen thousand, anyway," he muttered. "Darned inflated prices. Can't nobody afford to live in California these days."

"What in the tarnation are you mumbling about now?"

"I said when I get my share of the money, I'm moving to California. I'll be rich enough by then."

"Don't pack your bags yet, you fool. We still have to find it."

"Was anybody there?"

"I saw a fancy little sports car and a golf cart."

His brother perked up. "There's a golf course there? It's been a while since I've played a round of golf. Maybe we could—Hey! What'd ya hit me for?"

"Use that bloated head of yours for something other than a toboggan holder. We didn't drive thirteen hours from Kansas to Texas, just to play a round of golf. We came to get the gold that's rightfully ours. Our great-granddaddy stole that gold, fair and square!"

His brother balked at the choice of words. "Maybe it wasn't exactly fair..."

"Wasn't fair! He was a member of that gang, same as ole Sam Bass. Smarter than the outlaw, too. Outlived him by a lifetime, he did. Never once got caught."

"And never found the hidden gold, neither," his brother snorted.

"You better watch that smart mouth of yours, Delroy. Show some respect. You remember how Big Daddy used to talk about his own daddy. He worshiped the ground that man walked on. If he said he was a good man, he was a good man, so I'll charge you to show some respect for your ancestors! Big Daddy mourned his life away, trying to get justice for his old man. What better way could we show our respect than to be the ones to find that gold, once and for all? We could prove our great-granddaddy was as good an outlaw as any of the rest. Better, in fact, because he lived to brag about it!"

Del knew better than to speak out, else he would get another cuff to the head. It went without saying that if their great-grandfather bragged too much, he would have spent his last days in prison, or at the hands of some greedy bounty hunter. Probably the only reason their great-granddaddy lived to the ripe old age of seventy was because he was timid as a church mouse, and poor as one, too. Least ways, that was what Granny Thelma always said. She said her father-in-law robbed that stage on accident, and then made the mistake of throwing in with the likes of Sam Bass and his friends. Got a reputation as an outlaw, when the only thing he was guilty of was being ugly. Having a patch over his eye and a deep scar on his cheek—both the result of an accident as a teenager—only made matters worse.

Of course, there was one other thing he was guilty of. He lost the map. All because a pretty little German girl turned his head...

"Are you listening to me?" his brother asked in disgust.

"Sure, Bigs."

"No, you ain't. I can tell by the look in your eye, you were off daydreaming again! Gather your thoughts, man. You're a growed man, almost sixty years old, not some teenager. We have work to do. That gold has been hidden too long. The old woman had the map, and now she's dead. She was the last of the bloodline, so the curse on our family died with her. Ain't nothing standing between us and that gold now, little brother. It's ours for the taking."

Del bit his tongue. His brother meant it was theirs for the searching.

Like he said, they still had to find the treasure.

CHAPTER 8

True to his word, Walker brought dinner with him that evening.

After feeding the livestock, he and Hannah gorged themselves on the meal from Matousek's. Hannah wasn't a fan of beer in general, but the bottles of dark ale were a perfect accompaniment to the authentic German cuisine.

"That was insanely good." Hannah gave her mark of approval as she looked around the kitchen.

Leftovers stored, dishes washed, kitchen spotless. Along with the ready-made meal, Walker brought in a few more groceries and several packages of meat, which were now stashed and waiting for future consumption.

"Yes, it was." He offered the whole-hearted agreement with an emphatic air.

"Oh! I completely forgot to tell you," Hannah said, quite out of the blue. "I was so blown away by that meal, I forgot to tell you about my strange visitor today."

Busy stuffing the takeout containers into the trash and gathering the bag for disposal, Walker tossed a distracted, "Oh, yeah?" over his shoulder.

"I came in from exploring the other buildings and there was this random woman at the desk, trying to look through the guest ledger. The thing is, she was dressed really weird. Are there many neighbors living nearby? I think she walked here."

"There's a house down the road about a half mile. Maybe it was Mrs. Knudson. She wears a lot of baggy clothes and is a bit nosy, but she's a harmless little old lady. And you should taste her kolaches. Every bit as good, if not better, than the ones we just had, but still not as good as Sadie's."

Hannah shook her head. "This wasn't an old lady. She was young and very pretty, in a pale, china doll sort of way. She said her name was Caroline. And get this. When I turned my back, she snuck upstairs and somehow managed to get into one of the locked rooms."

Walker went perfectly still, his back to her. "You saw Caroline?" His voice sounded strained.

"You *know* her?" Hannah gasped. "Is she... all right? Mentally, I mean? She seemed rather... I don't know, disturbed. In a sad, tragic kind of way."

Walker cleared his throat and turned slowly around. "You met Caroline," he repeated slowly. It wasn't a question, it was a clarification. "You spoke to her."

"Yes. And then the weirdest thing happened. I still don't know how she did it, but somehow, she got from the second floor down to the outside of the inn. Is there a hidden staircase I know nothing about? A secret passage of some sort?"

Walker swallowed hard. "No hidden staircase."

"Then how did she do it? And why do you look so shaken up?" A thought suddenly occurred to her. Her eyes rounded into wide orbs. Her words came out breathless. "Is Caroline your *wife*?"

"What? No! Of course not! Caroline is... no. Not my wife." He shook his dark head in denial.

Hannah frowned. The attorney acted so strange. Suspiciously strange, in her opinion.

"What's her story, then?" she asked. "Who is she, and where did she come from? And what's with the costume?"

"Costume?"

"Yeah, some sort of hoop skirt, like a Southern belle might wear in *Gone with the Wind*." She used her hands to indicate the width of the domed skirt. "Oh, is there a historical park around here somewhere?" she guessed. "Like a working farm, where they dress in period clothing and demonstrate the old way of doing things? One of the firm's clients had a place like that." Her face scrunched into a frown. "Turned out they were using it as an illegal tax shelter. All the historical documentation was forged."

"The firm or the client?"

She shot him a dirty look but conceded. "Touché," she granted. She supposed it was a legitimate question, given the firm's notorious downfall. When he went back to tying up the garbage, Hannah persisted. "So? What's Caroline's story?"

It took him a moment to answer. "I think it's best to let her tell you that, herself."

Hannah huffed out her displeasure. "Do you know when she'll be back?"

"I'm surprised you saw her today," was his only reply. He hefted the bag over his shoulder. "Any other garbage I need to take out?"

She gave a dismissive wave. "None that I know of."

"If you're ready to go up, I'll lock up again tonight."

Apparently, the subject of Caroline was closed. She certainly wouldn't tell him about the crazy ideas she entertained today, concerning the town's future.

"Very well," she said, her voice stiff. "Good night, then."

"Good night."

At least there was a good internet connection. Hannah set up her laptop in the sitting room, atop the cozy little desk she discovered earlier in the day. Much to her surprise, the *Spirits of Texas Inn* was connected to the worldwide web. It made searching for information so much easier.

The first thing she looked up was the inn, itself. Her eyes widened when a website popped up. It appeared professionally designed and functional. She scanned the opening page, reading the initial description. According to this, Hannah, Texas was the perfect place for summer gatherings. They catered to families and small groups, with tailored stays from two nights to two months. The property was currently closed for construction, the site claimed, but would open in time for summer.

Hannah clicked on the booking calendar. Just as Walker promised, there were several rooms already spoken for in the near future. In amazement, Hannah clicked through the month of June. Already at half occupancy, and at a very fair price. Enough, she judged, to make a profit, but reasonable enough to attract guests.

She read the descriptions of each room and studied their photos. Right off, she spotted several things that needed improvement. Room 4, for instance, was much prettier than it appeared in the picture. There was no mention of its corner advantage, with natural light streaming in from two sides. Wasn't it Room 2 that had the pullout couch? Nothing about it in the description, just a nod to 'comfortable seating after a day of rock climbing and exploration.'

Clicking onto the cabins, Hannah was discouraged reading the lackluster descriptions. Why not play up the fact that the smaller of the two—the Hoffman Cabin, apparently—had impressive luxuries behind a rustic presentation? The Anheim Cabin was described as 'Sleeps four comfortably, six in close quarters. Tub, no shower. Family friendly.'

"Sounds absolutely forgettable," Hannah concluded. She jotted down ideas for jazzing up the descriptions. Made a note to take and upload new photos.

First, of course, she would need access to the website account.

Another note, of things to ask Walker.

Eventually, Hannah left the inn's website and did another search, this one for other resorts in the area. Dozens, if not hundreds, of sites populated the screen. Theirs wasn't even on the first two pages, she noted. She changed a few keywords, trying to narrow the offerings. By the time she requested wedding venues, significantly fewer came up. Adding words like 'dance floor,' 'all-inclusive,' 'country setting,' and 'farm animals' cut the number in half or less.

The possibilities were mind-boggling. Head spinning, Hannah knew she couldn't sleep, not until her mind slowed its frantic pace. A glass of iced water would help. A glass of wine might just provide the cure.

Too bad both were downstairs. To score either, she had to brave the unknown territory of the first floor at night.

She knew a light burned all night in the kitchen. Decent illumination spilled in from the porch lanterns. The space was far from pitch dark. But light casted shadows, and Hannah saw them everywhere she looked. They lingered behind every chair, hung from the rafters, gathered deep and murky in all the corners. Cell phone in hand, finger poised over the flashlight feature, Hannah hurried across the great room and into the kitchen. Shadows such as these definitely called for wine.

While she was down here, she reasoned, she might as well snag another poppy seed kolache.

She sank her teeth into the packy creation, savoring the sweet, yeasty roll. Some places tried to pass off an ordinary pig-in-a-blanket as a kolache. They wrapped a piece of link sausage in a bun and had the audacity to give it the same name as this melt-in-your-mouth delicacy. As pastries went, it wasn't even on the same realm.

Nothing compares to this, Hannah mooned, inhaling the very essence of the treat. It smelled almost as good as it tasted, and it tasted divine. This sweet-filled delight was Czech cuisine at its finest.

Lost to the wonders of flavors currently exploding on her tongue, she didn't notice the noise at first. She was halfway through the roll, washing it down with a sip of wine, when the sounds registered in her mind. Sitting aside her wine glass, she grabbed her phone and moved hesitantly forward. The noise seemed to be coming from the office, that small inner room behind the front desk.

Hannah hovered with uncertainty. Should she ignore the noise, or call Walker down to investigate? It could be something as harmless as a mouse, in which case she could only imagine the attorney's reaction. He would no doubt rib her unmercifully. Given the fact it was already after midnight, his response might very well be more angry than amused.

She could just peek around the door. Not the front entry, where she would be confined to the small check-in area. She would look in through the side door, where she could make a run for it down the hall. Mouse or man, she might need a good running start.

Armed with a half-eaten pastry, a cell phone, and a huge bluff of bravado, Hannah crept forward. This wasn't like one of those teenage slasher movies, she assured herself, the ones where the girl goes outside to see where the eerie glow is coming from. Those scenes never ended well. No, this was nothing like that. For starters, she was still inside the safety of the inn. And Walker was just upstairs, a call—or a scream—away.

She stopped long enough to scroll down to his number, ready to dial it if need be. Anything bigger than a mouse, and she was hitting that button.

Plan of action intact, she proceeded down the hall and up to the door. She eased the panel open, peeking into the room's dark depths. So far, so good. The desk looked normal. The chair was empty. From out here in the hall, nothing looked amiss.

She stepped over the threshold. Was that the sound again? She stood still and listened. Her eyes burned as she stared into the dark cavern and tried to determine the location of the noise. If it was a mouse, it wasn't scurrying around on the floor. It was more likely nibbling on paper, from the sounds of it.

Great. I still haven't looked through the ledgers or account books, and now a mouse is feasting on them. Another thing to ask Walker about. Pest control.

Hannah didn't see the mouse on the desk, but it had to be there. A large, leather-bound book lay open-faced on the side of the desk furtherest from her. It was too dark to decipher any details, but the pages of the book gave off that pale, eerie glow. *Nothing like the movies,* Hannah assured herself. *No one is ever murdered by a book.*

Something ruffled the page. *Must be a mouse,* she decided. *It looks like the page just turned, but that's impossible, unless the little critter somehow crawled underneath, pushed... Nah. Impossible. It only **looks** like it turned. Tricks of the night shadows.*

Feeling more confident, Hannah kept her eyes trained on the desk as she flipped the light switch. Maybe she could see how big of a rodent they were dealing with, or where it ran and hid. She was more repulsed by the hairy little creatures than she was afraid of them. The sooner they got rid of them, the better.

But even with her eyes steady on the book, she saw nothing scurry away with the sudden flood of light. Nothing moved, nothing made a sound. Hannah moved forward, peering over the side of the desk. Still nothing. She made a complete circle, seeing no signs of an unwanted guest. Not even a nibbled-upon piece of paper.

Chalking it up to her imagination, or perhaps exhaustion, Hannah shrugged her shoulders and reached for the light switch. As she plunged the room into darkness, she took a bite of her kolache. No need letting it go to waste.

Was it her imagination, or did she hear a faint rustle? Not of paper, but of fabric? Her hand flew back to the switch, but nothing moved in the room, once again illuminated. She walked all the way through this time, exiting on the far side. Nothing moved behind the check-in counter, either, nor in the shadowed great room beyond.

As she turned off the two-way switch, she thought she caught a faint whiff of lavender.

Forget the kolache and the wine. It was definitely time to go to bed.

CHAPTER 9

"I have a contractor coming out today, to give us a bid on turning the old store into a third cabin."

"I beg your pardon?" Hannah said, looking up from the bowl of oatmeal she doctored with brown sugar and granola. She paused before stirring in the fresh cream.

Walker had shown her how the cream rose to the top of the milk, just waiting to be scooped off and enjoyed. Fresh cream, she adored. The milk, not so much. It had been several days now, and she still hadn't acquired a taste for it.

Walker repeated his announcement as he dished out his plate of scrambled eggs and toast, next to his own bowl of oatmeal and a thick slice of country-style ham.

"And you did this without consulting me first."

Something in the quiet timbre of her words snagged his attention. He jerked his head up, just in time to see the flash of fire in her blue stare. His voice remained calm. "That's right."

"And why is that? As you are so fond of reminding me, I am the owner of this—this kingdom now!" She spread her arms wide, to indicate the whole of the outdated kitchen, wood stove and all. She waved toward the tiny town beyond. "Don't you think that was my decision to make, and mine alone?"

Not that she was opposed to the idea of another cabin. Ever since the crazy notion of improving and expanding had entered her mind, it was all she could think of. Truth be told, she was angry with herself for not thinking of this idea first. Turning the rundown old store into another rental cabin made perfect sense.

Still, he should have consulted her first.

Walker took his time, scraping out the last of the eggs and returning the skillet to the burner, making certain it was cool to the touch before doing so. "Perhaps your decision to make," he conceded, sauntering across the room to join her at the table. He settled into the chair, added salt and pepper to his eggs, and continued, "But not alone, it's not. I have a stake in this, too, you know. As executor of the trust, all major decisions and purchases have to go through me." He stirred a spoonful of peanut butter into his oatmeal. "Keep in mind, I'm not ordering any work done yet, and certainly not without your input. I'm merely gathering bids, so that when the time comes, we can make an informed decision. Together."

"You mean at the end of my thirty-day imprisonment."

"It's not an imprisonment."

"Says the man who is free to come and go at his leisure."

"Are you saying you want me to cancel the appointment?"

Surprised—and pleased—that he offered to do so, Hannah blinked in surprise. "Uhm, no. No, that won't be necessary."

He ruined the moment by flashing his most charming smile. "Then we don't have a problem, do we?"

The contractor drove a beat-up old truck with peeling paint and a slightly crooked, magnetic sign that identified his business as *Jobs Done Right*. Hannah thought he should have done a better job making his own first impression right. What if his rundown truck was a reflection of his workmanship? He might leave the cabin in worse shape than it was now.

Just the same, she followed Walker out to greet the carpenter. She wanted him to understand, right from the beginning, that he would be dealing with her, should he get the contract.

As the man crawled from the front seat of the truck, she felt Walker stiffen in surprise. "Who is that?" he muttered.

"Don't you know him? You're the one who called him!"

"I called Hank Ruby. That's not Hank."

They watched as a burly man stood outside the truck, preparing himself for the work ahead. He stuffed a pencil behind his right ear, tucked a measuring tape onto his cavernous overalls, and fumbled around on the dashboard until he came out with a clipboard. Adding a cap to his balding head and a flashlight to his pocket, he turned and saw he had an audience.

"Howdy, folks. Pretty place you got yourself here."

Hannah trotted alongside Walker, trying to match his purposeful stride as he greeted the man, more or less. His voice was as hard as steel. "I was expecting Hank Ruby. He and I spoke on the telephone yesterday."

"Ah, yeah, about that." The man scratched at his head and offered a sheepish smile. "The wife and I are down from Wichita Falls, visiting her family. Cousin Hank woke up deadly sick this morning, don't you know. Could barely lift his head off the pillow or his be-hind off the commode, if you'll pardon the reference, ma'am." He bobbed his head in Hannah's direction. "I have a contracting business myself, don't you know, so I offered to come for him. You don't mind, do you?"

Walker's hesitation was obvious. "As long as you take good notes and measurements," he slowly agreed, "I don't see why it would hurt." He extended his hand. "Walker Jacoby, Attorney at Law. And this is Hannah Duncan, owner of the property."

"Owner, eh? You and your husband, I reckon? Is he here, too?" The man craned his neck to look for him.

"I'm not married," Hannah said, taking an immediate dislike to the man. "I didn't catch your name."

"Pardon the manners. Harry's sudden sickness threw me for a loop this morning," the man chuckled. "Name's Tinker. Everett Tinker." He thrust out a big, sweaty hand that Hannah reluctantly shook.

"Harry?"

"No, ma'am, Everett. Everett Tinker."

"You said *Harry's* illness. I thought your cousin's name was Hank."

"Oh, right, right. It's a nickname my wife had for her cousin when they were kids. He had long hair, don't you know, back in the day."

Hannah wondered why Walker regarded the man with a frown. Perhaps he didn't like the contractor any more than she did.

The stranger didn't notice. He peered into the bright sun as he surveyed the property. "Which one of these buildings are we tearing down? Looks like they all pretty much need it."

"We aren't tearing down any of them. We're remodeling that third building there. But perhaps we should wait until Hank is feeling better." Walker's voice was tight.

"No, no, we're fine. I can get you fixed right up. I can even start the work tomorrow morning, don't you know."

"That won't be necessary. All we need today is a bid."

Everett Tinker looked disappointed. His eyes roamed over the town again, zeroing in on the old inn. "I reckon that one is next on your list. I can work up a bid on that one, too, don't you know."

"Again, that won't be necessary. Just the one." Walker's reply was cool and firm.

"Hey, you're the boss." The contractor flashed a big smile, revealing his aversion to dentists.

"Actually, Miss Duncan is the boss."

The man had the audacity to chuckle. "Well, sure, she is." He may as well have acknowledged she was the tooth fairy, for all the conviction in his voice.

Hannah stiffened immediately. Walker put a hand to her waist and leaned in to whisper, "Easy there, tiger."

Leroy came bounding up from unknown parts, none too happy to find a stranger in their midst. He barked wildly, charging right up to the man in baggy overalls.

"He—He don't bite, does he?" The large man visibly paled.

"Not with one of us around. But I don't recommend dropping by, unannounced," Walker was quick to warn. He reached out his other hand to quieten the dog. "Leroy. Sit."

The shaggy white beast obeyed the command with obvious reluctance. He growled low in his throat, just to state his position on the matter. Hannah leaned into Walker and whispered out of the side of her mouth, "I agree with Leroy."

The three of them walked down to the old storefront, Leroy close on their heels. Walker gave the carpenter a brief description of the work needing done.

Tinker squinted in the sunlight and stabbed a beefy finger toward the structure next door. "Might need to see one of the other cabins, don't you know, so's I can get a feel for what you're looking for."

After exchanging a look with Walker, Hannah shrugged and pulled out her keyring. Tinker grinned as they moved to the small cabin.

The carpenter poked through the space, opening doors and examining hinges, sliding out first one panel, then the next, testing the sturdiness of a wall or the bottom of a drawer. He had even looked under the bed.

"Mighty fine workmanship in here," he commented at last.

"Thank you," Walker said stiffly.

"Hank did this, did he?" When Tinker ran his hand under the edge of the bar, Hannah hoped he came out with a long, sharp splinter.

"As a matter of fact, I did this," the attorney replied.

Hannah and Tinker both snapped their heads in his direction. All Hannah could manage was a stunned, "You?"

Tinker, on the other hand, droned on about first one thing, and then another. He liked the sliding panel over the television. Were there other hidden surprises? He had suggestions for where the electrical panel should have been... where was it, by the way? Where was the main breaker box for the property, just in case he needed to know? Some old buildings had a false floor, or a lowered ceiling. What about these? Any crawl spaces he could know about?

"Let's look at the other cabin," Tinker suggested eagerly.

"Honestly, Mr. Tinker, all we're asking for is a bid on the old store." Walker glanced at his watch. "I have another contractor scheduled for two o'clock."

"Oh, well, sure, sure. I can be done by then, don't you know."

"Actually, I don't know," Walker replied smoothly. "Let's go find out, shall we?"

Hannah breezed past his outstretched arm, her grin stretched wide. For once, the lawyer's smirk was directed at someone other than her.

A trail of dust still hung in the air behind Everett Tinker's old truck. Hannah turned on Walker and charged, "I do *not* like that man!"

"That makes two of us." Putting a hand onto Leroy's head, he felt the great beast tremble with controlled energy. "Correction. Three."

"I wonder why Leroy kept barking like that, running back and forth between the inn and the store."

"He obviously didn't like Tinker, any more than we did."

"And what was with all the banging and tapping? We're going to tear down the inner walls and remodel. What's it matter if they're hollow or solid? And why are you still staring toward the road?" Following his gaze, a thought occurred to her. She instinctively moved a step closer and dropped her voice. "Do you not trust him to truly leave the property?"

"I don't trust him at all."

"Then why did you call him?"

"I didn't. I called Hank Ruby, remember?"

However, Hannah was on a roll, still peppering him with questions. "And why didn't you tell me *you* did that work in the cabin? The craftsmanship is amazing! Why do we even need a contractor? You could just remodel the old store."

He was too distracted to respond to her compliment. "Something doesn't add up."

"I know." Hannah sighed, deflating like a balloon. "You have a law practice. Not enough hours in a day to work on the building, too. It doesn't add up."

"No, not that. Well, yes that, but I was referring to Tinker. He said he was from Wichita Falls."

"So?"

"His truck has Kansas plates."

By silent accord, they turned and started toward the inn.

"Maybe he meant Wichita, as in Wichita, Kansas. Maybe he added 'Falls' by mistake."

"I admit, he's not the hottest burner on the stove, but surely he knows where he lives."

Hannah looked doubtful. After a moment, she brightened. "We don't need his bid, anyway. We have that other contractor coming at two."

Walker opened the inn door and held it for her, a mischievous smile playing on his lips. "There's no other contractor," he admitted. "I just told him that to hurry him along." With a wicked wink, he added, "Don't you know."

Hannah laughed along with him, but warning bells sounded in her head.

He's married. Married, married, married. He may have spent the last five nights here, helping you out and making you feel safe, not a wedding ring in sight, but he is OFF limits. No use in noticing his sexy laugh and his to-die-for smile. Get over it.

"I'll throw some lunch together," she offered, eager to get away from the smile she tried so hard to ignore. "Do you have time before you leave?"

She told herself she didn't notice the graceful play of muscles along his arm, either, when he consulted his wristwatch. "I should have time for a quick bite. If we have pork chops left from last night, I can warm one of those."

She nodded and hurried off to the kitchen.

Walker found her there a few moments later, staring into the refrigerator. She had plates and a tub of leftover potato salad on the counter, but no pork chops. He peered over her shoulder. "Where's the meat?"

"That's what I'd like to know!" She tossed him a suspicious look. "Was that you I heard last night, banging around in the kitchen? Did you get hungry and have a midnight snack?"

He backed away, palms offered up in a gesture of innocence. "I thought that was you down here."

"I have a strict policy about not wandering around in the dark." *Not after the other night*, she added silently. She took the empty platter from the refrigerator shelf and wagged it toward him. "If you didn't eat these, who did?"

"It must have been Leroy, because I'm telling you, I didn't eat them." He went so far as to frown in disappointment. "And I already had my taste buds all set for them."

"Leroy did not open this refrigerator and get out the pork chops. You did this, Walker Jacoby," she accused.

"I swear, I didn't eat the leftover pork chops. Scout's honor." He made an official-looking sign with his fingers.

Her blue eyes narrowed. "Were you ever a scout?"

"No, but that's beside the point. I still didn't eat the pork chops."

She merely huffed. "Looks like you're eating sandwiches, then."

"Fine with me. Hey, have you seen that folder I left on the check-in counter? I went to grab it just now, and it's not there."

"Haven't seen it."

"Hmm. Maybe I left it somewhere else."

Hannah fretted while she pulled together the makings for sandwiches. Carrying the offering to the table, she finally voiced her troubled thoughts.

"Walker? You don't think... I mean, surely she wouldn't... she seemed more sad than dangerous, but—but could *Caroline* have moved your file and eaten the pork chops? You don't think she somehow managed to get in, do you, and... and snooped around?"

He didn't answer right away. He seemed to give the idea serious merit before answering, albeit indirectly. "I'm certain Caroline didn't eat the pork chops," he assured her.

"How can you be so sure? Is she a vegetarian?"

He smiled at the very thought. "I doubt it. But trust me, Caroline didn't eat them."

Hannah wasn't fooled for a minute. "Because *you* did!" she accused.

"I did no such thing."

"Well, if you didn't, and Leroy and I didn't, and now you insist Caroline didn't, then who in the heck ate the pork chops?" Hannah demanded.

Walker stared toward the great room, and the front door beyond that. "I don't know," he admitted. His brows drew together in a frown. "I just don't know."

CHAPTER 10

"Like taking candy from a baby."

Delroy slipped into the front seat of the old pickup and held up a manila folder. His thin face split with a grin.

"What is that?"

"Some sort of contract. Lots of 'wherefores' and other such nonsense. It looked important, so I took it."

"What's in the other hand?" his brother asked, pulling away from the shoulder of the road. Del had been waiting in the trees, just as planned.

"That, dear brother," Del said, popping the last of the morsel into his mouth and smacking his lips, "was just about the best pork chop I ever did taste."

"I'm glad you enjoyed your midmorning snack," his brother jeered. "What else did you find? I stalled as long as I could, giving you more time to snoop."

"I couldn't snoop too much," Del complained, licking his fingers clean. "That woman was watching me."

"What woman? There ain't another woman out there. I've been casing the place all week, don't you know."

"Don't know how you could miss a fine woman like her. Long blond hair, skin as fair as day, a pretty yellow dress that hung all the way to the floor. Mighty fine-looking woman."

His brother flung his beefy arm out, walloping him in the chest. "I sent you in there to find something useful, you fool, not to flirt with the cook!"

"I found this, didn't I?" the younger man scoffed, waving the folder in the air triumphantly.

"What is it, then? What's it say? Does it have a copy of the map inside?"

"Well, let's just take a look-see and find out." Delroy opened the folder and scanned the first page. "It says here the party of the first part is demanding su—sufficient r—re—renumeration," he struggled with the words, "for concentration of expenses in—incurred—"

"You mean compensation."

"Yeah, that too." Del scanned the rest of the document, until he reached the last page. "Okay, here we go. This says that Opal Finke is demanding seven thousand and fifty-two dollars from *Hill Country Home Insurance*."

"Who the heck is Opal Finke?"

"The poor woman whose house flooded when the water pipe broke. Ouch! Whatdidya hit me for?" He shrank into himself, but he couldn't pull far enough away to escape his brother's wrath. Bigs slapped at him blindly, swatting anything his flapping arm came in contact with. The truck swerved a crazy path down the blacktop road. "Watch it, Bigs! You nearly run us off the road!"

"I'll not only run you off the road, I'll run you out of town!" Snatching the cap off his head, Bigs used it to extend his reach. He continued to swat at his brother, who now hovered against the far door. "I'll run you off the dad-blamed planet! That file you stole ain't got nothing to do with the hidden treasure, you idiot. That's just some old lady suing her insurance company. I swear, sometimes you ain't got a lick of sense!"

"Big Daddy always said it was the curse," Delroy defended himself. "The curse that little German gal put on our family, when Great-Granddaddy Patch didn't go back and marry her."

"You ain't cursed," his brother denied. "You're just plumb stupid."

CHAPTER 11

Humming along with the music streaming from her phone, Hannah studied the ledgers scattered in front of her. Fortunately for her, Miss Wilhelmina kept excellent documentation through the years, even though it was all done by hand. With nothing recorded electronically, Hannah had to search through each ledger, one by one. It was a slow process, but she was making progress.

She was buoyed by the totals in the margins. *The Spirits of Texas Inn* was, indeed, a profitable business, just as Walker reported that first day. It helped that a substantial deposit was made in late 1970, and again the following year. Smaller but still significant amounts followed for the next five years. With a healthy bank account to fall back on, the inn could afford a few lean times.

Most interesting of all was the fact that Miss Wilhelmina, like the innkeepers before her, made side notes throughout the ledgers. In many ways, the notes read like journals.

Some notes were brief and to the point: *Raining.* Or, *Construction on the new highway.*

Others gave a brief recap of guests, and events in the area. *Sweet couple, here for first anniversary.* Or, *Trail ride and reunion for Bottoms Family.* And, *Lecture at library over hidden treasure. Should get their facts straight.*

"Hidden treasure!" Hannah read aloud. "Knowing JoeJoe, that's the whole reason he bid on this crazy place." She blew away a tendril of dark hair that kept falling into her face. There was a bit of a draft in the room. "As if the man needs any more money," she grumbled. "He just loves the thrill of the hunt."

Despite his crazy, impulsive ways, she adored her uncle. He was the only family she had.

True, her mother was still living, but their relationship was hardly described as that of 'family.' They were more like polite strangers, exchanging Christmas cards and occasional texts. When was the last time she had heard from her mother in person, anyway? Sometime around husband number five, she thought. The producer who claimed he could revive her career and get her the type of leading roles she deserved. No more achy joint commercials and dowdy grandmotherly-type roles for the talented actress; she was a star, and he would help her shine. When that same husband and producer polished off her bank account a few months later, Jacqueline called her daughter. "Just to talk," her mother claimed, but Hannah knew the drill. Her mother only called when she needed something.

Back then, Hannah was in a position to help her mother when times got rough. With no one else to spend her hard-earned money on other than herself, Hannah could afford to be generous, in more ways than one. She would graciously overlook her mother's lack of parenting skills and send a note of encouragement after each hard-luck phone call. She always tucked a check in along with it, something to tide her mother over until her next big break came along.

Jacqueline called Hannah's father the dreamer, but it was she who lived in a fantasy world. Life in rural East Texas never suited the voluptuous brunette. She wanted something bigger, something better, than a wildcatter husband who worked in the oil fields. Even when it meant leaving her only child behind, Jacqueline could no longer resist the lure of fame and fortune. Terrell could chase his dreams of finding oil; Jacqueline had dreams of her own, and they led her to Hollywood.

Oddly enough, both realized their dreams, at the same exact time. *Duncan Drilling* hit a huge vein of oil, launching them into the big time, on the very day Jacqueline landed the role of Rhonda in *Doctors' General*, the most popular soap opera on television. With both of their careers spinning out of control, neither had time for an inquisitive little girl. Hannah bounced between the two of them like a ping-pong game that neither wanted to play. JoeJoe became the bright spot in little Hannah's life, the only person who ever seemed to have time for her.

Her uncle was just an overgrown kid, himself. Technically, he was a partner in Duncan Drilling, a business the two brothers inherited from their father. Terrell ran the company while JoeJoe finished his education and squandered his share of the profits on things like cheap women and expensive birthday presents for his only niece. By the time Terrell died in a rig explosion, the company was almost broke. Hannah inherited her father's share, but promptly sold it to her uncle. She wanted no part of the business, blaming it for taking her father's life and driving her mother away, all those years ago. One year later, her uncle was daring enough—or foolish enough—to throw in with an innovative new oilfield product coming out of Dubai. It made him an instant millionaire, several times over.

Now her uncle was a very *rich* overgrown kid, still buying extravagant gifts for his only niece.

Hence, here she sat, queen of her own little sad kingdom, reading over ledgers recorded in longhand.

The music began to cut in and out. Hannah picked up her phone and checked the signal. Something was playing havoc with the connection, causing interference.

Too bad, because the music kept the strange noises at bay.

A building as old and rambling as the inn made all sorts of odd and unexpected sounds. Nights were the worst, when silence settled in, broken only by the creak and groan of shifting seams and aging beams. And when Walker was away, and the house was empty save for her and Leroy, the noises came again, reminding Hannah of her isolation and her vulnerability. It was best to drown out the sounds with the radio, or Leroy's shuddering snores, or by whatever means she could find. Television, unfortunately, wasn't an option. The subscription to the satellite service had lapsed, and new equipment was required before the system could be restored. A technician wasn't scheduled until early next week.

Curious about the mention of a hidden treasure, Hannah typed it into her phone's search engine. The slow connection was excruciating. Deciding it was time for a break, she went upstairs to use her laptop. The inn's computer was password protected, and until the elusive Sadie and Fred returned, there was no getting in.

Hannah was surprised to read that, according to local legend, there was a hidden treasure buried somewhere in the nearby hills. In the late 1870s, notorious outlaw Sam Bass and a ragtag team of bandits perfected their robbery skills, targeting stagecoaches before moving on to the more modern—and lucrative—steam-powered locomotive. Most of their hits were smalltime efforts, executed more for experience than for wealth. However, legend had it that one of the stages carried covert cargo: two huge crates of gold and silver.

The Army was transferring a sizable fortune from Fort Worth to San Antonio. The plan was to send a decoy troop of soldiers by rail, armed to the hilt but in fact guarding empty crates. While attention was drawn to the pomp and circumstance of Army pageantry, the real gold traveled by stage, protected only by three undercover officers and the usual stage driver. The plan worked so well, two separate teams of bandits held up the train, fifty miles apart, and were taken into custody with minimal loss of life.

All went well until the stage neared the Hannah stop. As the vehicle neared South Grape Creek, a lone rider came up from the south and attempted to flag down the stage. Behind him, the Bass gang rode into view at the top of the hill, intent on overtaking that very same stage.

No one knew exactly what happened next. The only eye-witness left to tell the story was one of the officers, and he was in little shape to tell his tale. Best as anyone knew, fate played a cruel trick upon the men that day. When the officer grabbed his chest during the beginning stages of a heart attack, his fellow officers thought he had been shot. In the confusion, they over-reacted and assumed it was a robbery. Before Sam Bass and his gang made it down the hill toward the crossing, two officers and the driver were dead, the third officer was mistaken as such, and the lone rider was injured. The crates spilled out on the ground, revealing their fortune.

No one knew for certain how much money was at stake. The Army refused to give details. Some denied the freight was even on the stage to begin with; a blunder such as this didn't look good for their reputation. Bass and his gang, now plus one, were smart enough to keep their good fortune quiet. Right there at the creek crossing, they decided to hide the money and lay low. No need in spending a sudden unexplained fortune. When the time was right, they would return to the area and claim their booty.

Sam had success with a similar plan the year before, when he and the Collins gang robbed a train in South Dakota and got away with sixty thousand dollars in newly minted gold. After that heist, the men broke off in pairs, each with their share of the money. The poor fools who spent their money openly were now dead, while Sam, on the other hand, still rode free.

The lone rider from the stagecoach, injured and in need of care, entrusted his share to Sam. Even a poor farm boy from Kansas had heard of the great Sam Bass. He was known as a fair outlaw, if such a thing existed. To prove his trustworthiness, Bass drew a map, gave the only copy to the injured fellow, and took him to the nearest farmhouse, which just happened to be the stage stop. They concocted a story about the fellow being on the stage and injured when an outlaw rode up and robbed them, single-handed.

It was weeks before anyone knew the real story, or parts of it, at best. The surviving officer tried to set the record straight, but his speech was weak and slurred. He had difficulty relaying the conversation he overheard that day, about a band of outlaws hiding the gold. Eventually, it was determined that the injured man recuperating in Hannah was actually the lone outlaw. Before they could take him into custody, however, he somehow managed to escape. Most believed he had an accomplice, and some thought it was the young girl from the stagecoach stop, young Lina.

According to legend, the treasure was never recovered. While the lone rider recovered from his injuries, too weak to retrieve the gold, Bass and his gang rode into Round Rock, intent on robbing the bank there. The notorious outlaw was injured in a gunfight and died. People spoke of Bass' *other* hidden treasure, the money from the Dakota train robbery, but no one knew about the stagecoach heist. Not until the officer told his garbled story and the lone rider escaped in the night, never to be seen again.

Hannah read the story with a sense of mild amusement. Funny how rumors and legends came into being. If there were ever any hidden gold to begin with, the lone rider probably took it with him when he left the country. She supposed it was

more interesting, however, to imagine that it still hid somewhere in the hills, just waiting to be discovered. It was one of
those stories people told their kids, in random moments when
they had nothing else to talk about, or those times when they
wanted to distract them and pull their minds away from current circumstances. It was something to tell visitors to the
area, when there was little else to hold their attention. A fun
tale to recite around a campfire, or when one ran out of ghost
stories.

Hannah could definitely see her uncle falling for such a
ruse, caught up in the thrill and romance of the Old West legend.

"So much for that," she said, closing the website with a click
of her tongue. "If you ask me, legends of hidden treasure just
never seem to pan out. Stories like that are for dreamers." A
wicked thought occurred to her, and she giggled aloud. "And if
hell freezes over and my mother ever comes to visit, I'll share
the story with her. That might just be her best shot of getting
any money out of me these days. Alas, my well—therefore, her
well—runneth dry."

As Hannah descended the stairs, her mind went back to the
ledgers. She had spent the past few days studying them. Mention of hidden treasures aside, the books for the old inn
boasted a healthy bottom line. If staying captive for the full
thirty days meant a generous bonus for improvements and
remodeling, she might very well be sitting atop a hidden treasure of a different kind. The sort that required a little
imagination, a lot of hard work, and an investment of time and
energy. The kind that paid off in the long run.

Was she up to the challenge? Hannah pondered the enormity of the question as her foot hit the last step. This meant making a commitment. This meant no wiggling out of the contract terms. This meant no quitting in a year, even after she earned the second bonus.

And that sound she heard meant someone was in the kitchen...

Hannah picked up the pace.

CHAPTER 12

She rounded the corner, thinking she would see Walker, at best. Caroline—or perhaps Everett Tinker, don't you know—at worst. She never expected to see a beggar.

"Who—Who are you!" she demanded, seeing the strange man in the kitchen. He wore a ragged, dusty suit of clothes that had seen better days, with a floppy-brimmed western-styled hat and a bandanna at his neck. He looked as surprised as she did, his eyes wide.

"Name's Varela, ma'am." He tilted his head in a polite bow.

"How did you get in here?" Highly suspicious of him, Hannah darted her eyes around the room.

"I never meant for you to see me, miss."

"Why are you in here?" Hannah's voice rose in panic. "Are you robbing me?"

"Robbing you? No, no. No, ma'am, Orlan Varela is no thief." He bowed deeply, as if to prove his words with the polite gesture. This time, she detected a Spanish lilt in his rusty voice.

"If you don't explain yourself, right this instant, I'm calling 9-1-1." Her voice was still high with emotion.

"Please, ma'am, do not be upset. I'm friendly."

"You have no business being in the kitchen!"

He wore a sheepish expression upon his face. "It smells so good in here," he admitted.

Something in Hannah softened, but her guard was still up. "Did—Did you take the pork chops?" she asked.

The intruder was clearly confused. "The pork chops? No, ma'am, I am afraid not."

He sounded so sad. Mournful, in fact. It occurred to her that the man could be hungry and looking for food. She took a closer look at him, noting he was frightfully thin. "When was the last time you ate?" she asked.

"I could not say."

Praying she wasn't making a mistake, Hannah told him, "If you'll go out to the dining room, I'll bring you a sandwich. I'm afraid I'll have to ask you to leave after that. Take the sandwich with you."

"I do not ask for your food, ma'am."

"I'm offering."

"You are a kind lady."

Hannah edged away from him, making certain she was well out of arm's length as he came toward the doorway that led into the hall and out to the great room. She skirted along the far side of the kitchen, keeping her eyes trained on the back door, judging the distance, should she need to break and run.

And where, her racing mind screamed, was Leroy? He hadn't even barked, alerting her to the man's presence.

"I mean you no harm," the man told her, nonplussed by her avoidance of him.

"Wait out there," she repeated, already regretting her offer. "I'll bring your sandwich."

The moment he was out of sight, she dialed Walker's number. "Do you ever pick up!" she wailed, when the phone just rang and rang. She slammed it down as she rummaged through a drawer, looking for a knife. A nice, long, sharp butcher knife. She kept it by her side as her trembling hands prepared a sandwich.

She tried Walker's number again as she carried the food from the kitchen, wrapped in a plastic baggie. The butcher knife hid in the dishtowel she carried. As Walker's voicemail picked up, she stepped into the great room, eyes searching the empty space for her hungry and dusty guest.

"Mr. Varela?" she called. She hated the warble she heard in her voice. "Orlan? I—I have your food."

Great. Now she couldn't reach either man.

At the mention of food, Leroy came trotting forward. Hannah was relieved to see the shaggy giant as she called the beggar's name again. When still he didn't answer, Hannah looked for the man. He being in the kitchen was bad enough. Being in the office or behind the front desk was quite another, and completely unacceptable.

He was in neither place. Hannah had a sinking feeling. He *was* robbing her! He was upstairs this very moment, rummaging through her things, looking for anything of value.

Hannah dialed Walker's number again, to no avail. After a moment's hesitation, she dialed 9-1-1 and reported a trespasser. She told the dispatcher the person might possibly be robbing her.

"Ma'am, I want you to leave the property." The dispatcher spoke in a slow, clear, concise voice. "Can you do that?"

"Yes. Well, no, not completely."

"What do you mean, ma'am? Is the man preventing you from leaving? Is this a hostage situation?"

"No, nothing like that. It's... complicated."

"Ma'am, do you know the man who's in your house? Is this a domestic dispute?"

"No, I've never seen him before in my life!"

"If you're able to, I want you to exit the house," the dispatcher repeated calmly. "Exit the property, if at all possible."

"I can go outside." Hannah bobbed her head up and down, even though the person on the other end had no way of seeing.

"Are you there alone, miss?"

"I have Leroy with me. He's a dog. A really *big* dog."

"Good. That's good. Did he engage with the suspect?"

Hannah frowned. "No. As a matter of fact, he didn't even bark."

"Could you describe the intruder, ma'am? I've dispatched a deputy to your location, but it may take him several minutes to reach you. At least fifteen minutes, I'm afraid. In the meantime, please tell me everything you can about the perpetrator."

"He was about thirty," Hannah began. She wracked her brain, trying to recall the details she had been too frightened to notice. "Hispanic, I think, or at least a descendant. About five feet seven, and very thin. He—He wore brown cloth pants, like—like wool, or something. A brown-checkered shirt. And an old floppy hat."

"It sounds like you're describing a scarecrow, ma'am," the woman said, her tone slightly reproachful.

"No, more like an Old West cowboy. A—A vaquero. He had a bandanna around his neck and a..." her voice trailed off, as she all but whispered, "...a gun belt around his waist."

"A gun belt?" the woman squeaked. "The suspect is armed? Why didn't you say so!"

Hannah shook her head, suddenly getting a sinking feeling in her gut. "No, I don't think so. I—I'm sorry, I think I made a mistake. I think this man may work at the history farm. Leroy didn't bark. N—Never mind. I think this man may be a friend of Walker's."

The woman's voice brightened. "Walker Jacoby?" she chirped.

Hannah gasped. "You know him?"

"Know him? I've been half in love with him, most of my life!"

The sinking feeling reached her toes. "You're his wife?" Hannah whispered.

"Wife? Wife! Walker Jacoby's wife? Now that's a good one!" The dispatcher laughed, the sound deep and throaty. "I could only wish!"

Hannah stared at the phone. In the few and rare times she had need to call 9-1-1 in Houston, she had never once engaged in a personal conversation with the dispatcher. It seemed highly unprofessional, and borderline unethical. She cleared her throat.

Effectively brought back on task, the dispatcher asked, "You say you want me to call off the deputy?"

Hannah nodded, but, again, the woman couldn't see her. "Yes," she managed to say. "I'm sorry to have bothered you."

"Oh, no problem, honey. We're here for you, anytime. Tell Walker Tracey Ann said hey."

Hannah went back into the house and called Orlan's name again. Silence greeted her. She waited at the foot of the stairs for him to come down. Five minutes ticked by.

After another five minutes of indecision, she started up the steps.

There was no sign of the man in any of the rooms. Nothing appeared to have been disturbed. Hannah came back down and searched through the first floor. She saw nothing.

If not for the sandwich, the entire episode might have been a figment of her imagination.

"I see you called." Walker returned her call as she fed the last of the abandoned sandwich to Leroy. "I'm sorry, I was in an area with no cell service. Is something wrong?"

"Not anymore. But I wish you'd warn me when someone is dropping by."

His voice sharpened. "Did Tinker stop by?"

"Tinker? No, and I hope he doesn't! And certainly when you're not here!"

"I've asked him to drop his bid off here at the office. I don't want him back on the property, any more than you do."

"Did you tell his cousin how you felt? He really shouldn't have sent him in his stead, not without talking to you first."

"I've tried to reach Hank several times, but he doesn't answer."

"I guess he was really sick, then," Hannah said, feeling empathy toward the man. It was bad enough, just having a virus. Having a virus *and* a guest like Everett Tinker was a double whammy.

"If I don't hear from him in a day or so, I'll drop by and check on him. Hopefully his relatives will be gone by then."

"If they can remember where they live," Hannah snickered. "We've narrowed it down to either Wichita, Kansas, or Wichita Falls, Texas. We think."

"Again, not the sharpest tool in the shed," Walker said dryly. "But if Tinker didn't drop by, who were you referring to?"

"Orlan Varela. Tell me something. Do all your friends work at that history farm? Other than Tracey Ann. I know she works for 9-1-1. She said to tell you 'hey,' by the way. And where is that history farm, anyway? I can't find a thing about it on the internet."

Walker was quiet for a long moment. He finally responded to her questions, in random order. "How do you know Tracey Ann Porter works at the sheriff's office? Why were you talking to her?"

"Because I called 9-1-1 when your friend Orlan stopped by here to raid our refrigerator!" Her tone revealed her displeasure. He should have told her to expect the man, instead of allowing him to scare her half to death. "He said it wasn't him," she continued, "but I bet he's the one who ate the pork chops yesterday. Does he do this often? Stop by and raid the refrigerator, I mean?"

"H—How would I know?" Walker sputtered. "I don't live there!"

His answer gave her pause. "Oh. That's right," she murmured. "I keep forgetting. You're just here to babysit me."

She could hear the frown in his voice. "I wouldn't use the word babysit, Hannah. It's not like that."

Another thought occurred to her. "Maybe he's not your friend, after all. But he was clearly Miss Wilhelmina's friend. He knew his way around the kitchen, and Leroy didn't even bark at him."

"What was he doing?" Walker asked, his tone oddly hesitant.

"Nothing, really. I thought he wanted food, so I made him a sandwich. But while I was on the phone with Tracey Ann, hearing how she's been in love with you most of her life, he disappeared on me." This time, the frown appeared in her voice. "The people who work at that history farm are rather rude, aren't they? They just come and go at their leisure, walking in and out of here like they own the place!"

When Walker made no reply, Hannah scowled. "Well? Don't you have anything to say?"

"Uh... Tracey Ann was just joking. She's engaged to my friend Reece."

"Well, don't tell this Reece fellow, but if you weren't already taken, I think she'd rather be engaged to you."

He quickly changed the subject. "I think I might bring home pizza tonight. How's that sound?"

It was on the tip of her tongue to tell him not to bother. That he should take the pizza home, all right, to the house he shared with his wife. However, she remembered how easily Orlan had come into the inn, without her even knowing it. If he and Caroline came and went at will, were there others? She remembered all the strange noises, and the supposed mouse from the other night.

Sending the attorney home was the right thing to do.

But she wasn't quite brave enough yet.

"Pizza sounds fine," she said quietly.

CHAPTER 13

It was a nice day out, and Hannah suffered from cabin fever. It seemed the perfect time to do some yard work.

"This imprisonment is getting to me," she admitted aloud, if only to herself. Never one to handle a rake and hoe in Houston, she put both to good use on this fine day.

Someone, most likely the Tanners, kept the flowerbeds around the old inn tidy and clean, but straggly new weeds called attention to the couple's absence. Hannah plucked the unsightly reminders away and raked the ground around them, restoring beauty and order to the simple garden. Alternating a swing of the hoe with the sweep of the rake, she worked her way across the yard and to the other side of the gravel driveway.

By the time Walker arrived, she had hacked her way to the weeds that skirted the dance hall like fringe. She took a grateful break, resting her arm on the handle of the hoe and pushing away her sweaty hair. "Is it that late already?" she asked in surprise.

"No, I'm early."

She took one look at his solemn expression and muttered, "This can't be good." She nodded to the opened door of the old saloon turned dance hall. "Let's go inside. I have water."

Two water bottles, one of them untouched, sat on one of the long tables nearest the door. Eager for a chance to rest, Hannah took a seat on the simple bench running alongside the table. She offered him the unopened water as she took a long draw of refreshment from her own.

"It's not good," he concurred. "When I couldn't reach Hank Ruby yesterday, I decided to drop in on him. It's not like Hank to ignore a phone call, even when he's under the weather."

"And was he? Under the weather, I mean?"

"In a manner of speaking. He's dead."

"What?"

Walker's nod was sad and slow. "When he didn't come to the door, I walked around back and found one of the windows bashed in and the back door unlocked. I found Hank inside. From the looks of it, he had been dead for at least a couple of days."

"That's terrible." Even though she didn't know the man, she hated to hear of anyone's untimely death. "He must have been truly sick, to die so suddenly."

"That tends to happen when you're on the wrong end of a bullet."

"A bullet!" she gasped. "You mean—"

Walker interrupted her, his voice flat. "I mean he was shot to death. Apparently, someone broke into Hank's house, killed him, and left by way of the back door."

"Did you call the police?"

Clearly offended, Walker scowled at her. "What kind of question is that? Of course I called the police."

Hannah's hands fluttered in the air. "I'm sorry, of course you did. I'm just so surprised. A bit shocked, actually, though I don't know why. I didn't even know the man." She huffed out a sigh and admitted, "I guess I didn't think things like that happened out here."

"Like anywhere else, where there are people, there are crimes. Luckily, however, murder is few and far between."

"Murder!"

He gave her a sardonic look. "Of course murder. Did you think this was a friendly killing?"

"No, but... What about his family that was visiting? Everett Tinker and his wife. Were they already gone?"

Walker plopped down on the bench and reached for the water bottle. If he had been wearing a tie, he would have loosened it. Instead, he used one hand to free the top two buttons of his monogrammed western shirt, while with the other, he lifted the water to his lips. He guzzled half the bottle, but as he wiped his mouth with his palm, his hand lingered. Hannah imagined it was to steady his nerves. After all, he had just discovered a dead body.

Friend or not, it couldn't have been pleasant, particularly after two or more days.

"I don't think Everett Tinker was who he said he was," Walker admitted, his voice gravelly. "Something about his story just never made sense to me."

"Like what?"

"To begin with, I knew it wasn't like Hank to send someone else to do his bids for him. He would have at least called to ask if I minded, sick or not. And that bit about the nickname. I've seen pictures of Hank when he was young. Even way back when, he always wore a buzz." Walker drummed his fingers on the table, staring off into space. "I should have asked more questions. Hank never mentioned family in Kansas. I should have listened to my instincts and found out more about the man before I let him on the property!" He slapped the table, clearly angry with himself.

"You didn't know, Walker."

"But I should have! The man was too slick. Too eager. He wanted to start ripping things apart, the very next day. Asked too many nosy questions, too, wanting to know if there were false floors and where the breaker pole was, and if he could go in all the buildings. He was looking for something."

"Did you tell the police about him?"

"Yes, and there's no Everett Tinker in Wichita Falls *or* in Wichita, Kansas." He snorted in disgust.

"He had a magnetic sign on his truck," Hannah remembered. She snapped her fingers in repetition, trying to recall the name she had read. "Now what was it?" she murmured.

"*Jobs Done Right*," Walker supplied. "Which happens to be the name of a business over in Comfort. While they were doing a job here a few days ago, someone swiped the magnetic sign off their truck."

Hannah sucked in a sharp breath. "You don't—You don't think *Everett Tinker* killed your friend. Do you?" She added the last breathlessly.

"First of all, I don't think Everett Tinker is his real name."

She raised worried eyes to his. "And second?"

Walker's own eyes were a stormy blue. "I think there's a good chance he might have killed him, or at least he might know something about Hank's death. The last time anyone remembers seeing Hank was four days ago, when he told his buddies down at the diner about heading out here the next morning. My guess is that the man calling himself Everett Tinker overheard the conversation and took advantage of it. I think he got Hank out of the way so that he could show up here, instead."

Biting into her lip, Hannah remembered something the man had said. "It did strike me as odd, the way he claimed Hank woke up 'deadly' sick. Then again, everything about the man struck me as odd." She nibbled on her lip some more. "Why would he do that? Why would he want the handyman out of the way?"

"I'm not sure, but the man was up to something. He came here with a stolen sign, a false name, and a questionable story. I don't mean to alarm you, Hannah, but you need to be extra careful out here. Even if it turns out the man had nothing to do with Hank Ruby's death, he was definitely up to no good."

Hannah bounced up from the bench, like a ball of nervous energy. "Why would you tell me something like that? Now I'll be a total wreck! It's bad enough I can't leave the property; now I'll be too afraid to leave the inn. I truly will be a prisoner here!" she wailed.

"Leroy will protect you. He didn't like the man. He'll alert you if he tries to step foot on the property again."

She didn't look convinced. "When did you say the Tanners will be back?" She wasn't sure the older couple could offer much protection, but she would feel better having someone else around during the day. The so-called carpenter had been curious about a husband, so having a man around, even one that was likely to be pushing seventy, was a welcomed addition.

"Sunday evening," Walker assured her. "That's only three days away. I'll be here most of the day on Sunday, so it's really only two days you'll be here alone." Seeing her deeply puckered brow, he quickly amended his words. "One and a half, at best. I'll have a short day Saturday."

She was nibbling her lip again. "You said most of Sunday. Are you picking them up at the airport, or something?"

"No, I was referring to church." He gave her a sheepish look. "I'm sorry you can't go with me, but according to the terms..."

"I know, I know," Hannah said with a sigh. "The terms of imprisonment."

CHAPTER 14

With no sign of the unwanted carpenter, the next two days passed uneventfully. Hannah stayed indoors, studying the ledgers and making a few spreadsheets of her own. Lists, after all, were her specialty.

On Sunday morning, before Walker left for church, she managed to milk Buttercrunch by herself. The experience wasn't quite as much fun as it was when Walker guided her hands with his, but it was every bit as exhilarating.

Who would have ever guessed that Hannah Duncan, daughter of famed actress Jacqueline Duncan and niece of oil mogul Joseph Duncan, could find such satisfaction in milking a cow? But this was something she had done on her own, without help from her family. She coaxed out at least a dozen good, solid squirts before handing the task over to Walker.

She was pacing herself, she said. Starting slow so that she could get a good handle on things, no pun intended. The attorney laughed and took over the chore as she went off to gather eggs, also by herself.

A smile lingered on Hannah's face. Almost two weeks into her thirty days, and here she was acting like a farm girl. When Sadie and Fred Tanner arrived home this evening, they would never guess she was a greenhorn.

To welcome the couple back, Walker suggested a tailgate barbecue. It promised to be a beautiful evening, perfect for dining outside, and the Tanners loved surprises. He could grill a steak for Fred and fresh-caught fish for Sadie. In one of her weaker moments, Hannah agreed.

It was becoming more and more difficult to keep an emotional distance from Walker Jacoby. Not only was the man maddeningly attractive, but when he wasn't smirking at her, he could be downright charming. He had a sharp, witty sense of humor. Worst of all, there was no denying the man was actually rather *nice*. He pulled his share of the household chores, never pried into her past, gave Hannah her space, and most importantly, spent his nights here at the old inn so that she felt safe. If it put a strain on his marriage, he never let on.

She knew that having a bit of fun and relaxation this evening was a bad idea, even if they had the older couple there as chaperones. It was almost as if she and Walker were hosting the event, one couple to another. When Sadie called to say their flight was delayed and they were staying over until morning, Walker suggested they go ahead with the barbecue, just the two of them. She had the opportunity to back out. But the steaks were already defrosted, and she convinced herself that being in the wide, open outdoors was better than being in the confines of the house with the handsome attorney. Particularly after being cooped up in the house for two days, the call of the outdoors beckoned.

So here they were, down by the pond, and Hannah was the most relaxed she had been in recent memory. Far longer ago than twelve days.

Walker had loaded a small grill in the back of his truck and had driven to the pond, where they set up makeshift accommodations. He grilled two fat, sizzling steaks to perfection, while Hannah pulled together the rest of the meal. They ate on a card table in the middle of the field, with the ducks and geese to serenade them. Bluebonnets scented the evening air.

And now, with the cooking paraphernalia stashed away and the sun setting low on the horizon, they settled their chairs near the water's edge and shared a bottle of pre-chilled wine. Hannah's head lolled on the canvas back of the camp chair as she enjoyed the gentle breeze. It played in the dark silk of her hair, mussing it beyond redemption, but she couldn't muster up the strength to care. Only when it tickled her face did she lift a hand to push it away.

This country life was oddly addicting. In as little as twelve days, she had come to love the peace of a quiet spring night. She loved the sounds of nature around her, the feel of fresh air blowing across her skin. Most evenings, she sat out on her balcony and absorbed the magic.

But this, with the breeze off the water and the splash and sputter of the playful fowl, was so much better. Hannah sighed aloud with pleasure.

"Enjoying yourself?" Walker asked in an amused voice.

"Mmm. Yes."

Not that she would ever admit as much to her uncle, should he ever return her calls. JoeJoe was a royal pain when he gloated. It was just as well that he continued to ignore her.

"You're really getting the hang of working with the animals. I think we might make a country girl of you yet."

She lifted one eyelid. "Don't get ahead of yourself, big boy," she warned.

He chuckled, and the sound did strange and wicked things to her much-too-relaxed body. She made a half-hearted effort to scoot her chair further from him. They were close enough now that she could easily detect the deliciously mingled notes of charcoal, steak, and cologne upon his skin. It was a heady combination.

Married, she reminded herself.

"I'll be sure and tell Sadie and Fred what a fine job you're doing. They'll be pleased to have the help."

She wanted to ask what time the couple arrived in the morning, but it required more effort than she was willing to exert.

"Are you asleep over there?" he queried.

She didn't bother opening an eye. "Would be, if you'd quit talking."

"Pardon me," he chuckled.

She made it sound like such a good idea, he decided to try it for himself. The sun slipped further away, casting soft shadows into the twilight, and they both drifted into a peaceful state of unconcern.

The leg of Hannah's chair sank further into the sand, pressing against the soft earth with slow and gradual descent. The transition was so faint she never noticed the shift. When it finally gave way, the chair turned sideways and dumped her, unceremoniously, upon the sandy bank. She went down with a loud 'plop!' and a startled yelp.

The ruckus jarred Walker from a peaceful daze. "Hannah! Are you all right?"

He scrambled to sit upright, but his long legs tangled with the shorter legs of the folding camp chair. It began to collapse with him, spilling him into the sand beside her. He tried to avoid the collision, but his right side came down hard upon her.

"Ow! Get off me, you big oaf!" she complained, pushing at him to move.

But as they both began to laugh, their efforts became clumsy. Combined with the effects of the wine and the lazy trance that fogged their senses, their leaden limbs refused to cooperate. They collapsed into a tangled heap, laughing and winded, and both too dazed, or too comfortable, to move.

"Wh—What happened?" Walker finally managed to ask.

"My—My chair!" Hannah laughed too hard to make sense. "Sand. Fell. Pl—Plop!"

Another round of hoots, another hilarious attempt to pull apart. Another surrender to laughter.

Walker finally managed to move off her, his body angled to lie in the sand beside her. His hand was still slung over her waist.

"What a rude awakening!"

Hannah could feel the laughter in his voice. It echoed along her entire body, pressed against him as she was. She turned to make a smart remark, only to find his face was mere inches from her own.

His blue eyes darkened, as the air between them stilled. Maybe neither of them moved. Maybe they both did. A magnetic force pulled between them, drawing them together. Walker's eyes dropped to her mouth, his intentions to kiss her quite clear within the darkening blue depths. Hannah watched his lips part, felt the warmth of his breath against her face as he leaned in. She felt her body kindle and come alive, arching toward him as it took on a mind and spirit of its own. Her mouth watered, anticipating his kiss.

No! her mind screamed, and not a moment too soon.

Hannah pushed up and away, banging her shoulder into his face in the process. As she crawfished backward and put a safe distance between them, Walker howled in pain and nursed his busted nose.

"What in the—" He bit back the curse as blood dripped into his hand. "You busted my nose!"

"You tried to kiss me!" she accused.

He gave her a dark look over his cupped palm. "A simple no would have been sufficient," he told her dryly.

"How dare you! How dare you just sit there, acting so nonchalant? What would *Mrs.* Jacoby say about what you just did?" Hannah demanded.

He looked at her as if she spoke Italian, a language he didn't understand. "What does she have to do with this?"

"What! Oh! Oh, you—you—you cad!" Steam all but came from her ears. In her fury, Hannah scooped up a handful of sand and flung it at him.

"And you are the orneriest woman I have ever known! I try to kiss you, and first you bust my nose, then you throw sand in my eyes. What is wrong with you?"

"Wrong with me! Wrong with *me*? You're the one who has no business kissing me! You're the one with a wife at home!" She flung the words as violently as she had flung the sand.

Walker grew perfectly still. The look on his face was pained.

"Hannah." Something in the gravel of his voice made her look up. Made her listen. "I'm not married."

She lost some of her starch. "It's okay, Walker. I know," she told him quietly. She was suddenly very weary. She had been fighting this for an entire week, this unhealthy attraction toward him. It was almost a relief, getting it all out in the open. It was hard to fight demons that hid in the closet. Best to meet them head on, and attack. "I figured it out. You and your wife are going through a rough patch, and you need a place to stay, a place that gives you both the space you need. I get it. But this—" she waved her hand in the few feet that separated them "—this isn't going to happen."

"Hannah," he said, voice deceptively calm, "there's something you need to know."

She held up a stalling hand. "In my book, separated is the same as married."

"Agreed." He wiped at his nose, saw no blood, and hesitantly lowered his hand. With the other hand, he scrubbed the back of his neck, avoiding her eyes. "The thing is..." His blue eyes finally met hers. "Hannah," he said slowly. "I am not, nor have I ever been, married."

Was he speaking German? She saw his lips moving, but the words didn't make sense.

"But... who's Mrs. Jacoby?" she asked in confusion. "That first day I met you, you said, 'Mrs. Jacoby' was of a like mind as me, in that she didn't need a man to make decisions for her."

"And she doesn't," he agreed in quick time. "My mother is a strong, independent woman, just like you."

"Your—Your *mother*?"

"Yes, the woman married to my father. That makes her Mrs. Jacoby. Mrs. Sarah Jacoby, to be exact, wife of Andrew Jacoby."

If he expected to see relief in her eyes, he was sadly mistaken. Her blue eyes kindled with ire. Once again, she fisted a handful of dirt, but this time when she threw it, it was in the opposite direction, although with equal force.

"Argh!" she bit out her displeasure. "All this time, you let me think you were a married man! Let me berate myself, for being attracted to you! Do you know what you've put me through? You're... You're despicable!" she spat.

He had the grace to hang his head in shame. Until that moment, Hannah hadn't noticed that the sun was completely down. In its place, a full moon hung in the sky, doubly bright as it bounced off the waters. When Walker raised his head again, she had no trouble seeing his face, and the pained expression upon it.

"I didn't know you thought I was married. Honest. But yes, I do know what you've been going through. I've been going through the same thing."

When she frowned in confusion, he explained, "You were right, Hannah. This—" he waved his hand between them, just as she had done moments ago "—can't happen. You're my client. It would jeopardize our professional relationship and perhaps my ability to make impartial and sound business decisions on your behalf. Exploring our attraction to one another wouldn't be wise."

Although she agreed with what he said, it still hurt to hear the words, particularly when he said them with such a formal air.

"I couldn't agree more." She forced the words to come out naturally, hoping they didn't sound as brittle as they felt.

"Good. I'm glad we've cleared that up."

"Me, too."

They sat in awkward silence, each studying an opposite line of sight, until Hannah finally spoke, her voice small. "I'm sorry about your nose."

"If I really were a married man, I would have deserved as much, and more."

She pointed out the obvious. "But you aren't really a married man."

"And for that, I apologize. Not for being single, but for any misunderstanding between us in that regard."

Hannah waved her hand dismissively. "Water under the bridge. And if my stupid chair hadn't collapsed, I'd be none the wiser."

Even in the moonlight, she could see his mouth twitch in humor. "You have to admit, that was pretty funny. One minute you were all but snoring, the next you were lying there in the sand, like a forgotten rag doll."

She raised her nose and sniffed. "I do not snore."

"Sure sounded like it to me."

"Humph! How dare you!" Her words lacked heat. She tossed another handful of sand, this one to land harmlessly on his jean-clad thigh.

He brushed it carelessly away. When his eyes met hers, they both broke out in laughter, recalling those earlier moments in the sand. By the time the laughter died away, a tentative truce had formed between them.

"So, tell me more about Hannah Duncan."

"What's to tell? I thought I had a bright and lucrative career as a senior assistant in one of the top investment firms in the state, if not the country. I couldn't have been more wrong."

"And before you were a senior assistant?"

Her brow knitted together as she tried to remember a time before she worked for *Lawrence, Schuster, and McMahon Investments.* "I guess I was in high school, working for *Duncan Drilling.* When I was in college, David Lawrence gave me an internship at the firm, and I never left." Hannah drew a pattern in the sand with her fingers. "That makes me sound awfully boring."

"Or awfully dedicated. That's a rare trait these days, Hannah."

"For all the good it did me."

"So, what about you? Have you ever been married?"

"Who had time for marriage?" She scoffed at herself. "I barely had time to attend my friends' weddings. All of them, by the way, are now married. I'm the odd woman out."

"I know what you mean. Most of my friends are married, engaged, or recently divorced. I'm basically the same thing. Odd man out."

Hannah pursed her lips and pretended to sulk. "Well, aren't we the sorry lot?"

They engaged in idle chitchat, enjoying the night air that played around them. Walker poured them more wine and they resurrected their chairs, making certain the feet were firmly planted in the edge of the grass. They faced the pond, both enjoying the same view this time, and peacefully so.

After a while, Hannah made a quiet announcement. "I've decided to stay."

He looked at her in surprise. "There was a doubt? You have almost two full weeks whipped. You're doing great."

"I don't mean just through the thirty days. I mean I've decided to stay, permanently. I have some ideas I'd like to implement for the property. To help it grow and be more successful."

"That's great."

"You don't sound very convincing. I thought you'd be pleased."

"I am."

His strained reply stung. They may have agreed not to have a personal relationship, but she had hoped for some sort of friendship, at the very least.

"Stick with your lawyer gig," she advised dryly. "You'd make a terrible actor."

"It's not that. I'm really glad you're thinking in terms of the future, Hannah, and that you're planning to stay."

By now, she was clearly agitated, and she didn't mind letting him know. "I hear a definite 'but' in your voice."

Walker's internal struggle was obvious. He warred with himself for a long moment before he released a sigh and scrubbed the back of his neck. Hannah was quickly coming to dread that particular telltale action.

"There's something I've been meaning to tell you, Hannah…"

Before he could continue, Leroy shot to his feet and barked. He faced the direction of the inn, his entire body on alert.

"What's up, boy? What do you hear?" Walker asked.

The shaggy white beast ran forward, only to return a few moments later, barking excessively.

"What it is, Leroy?"

The dog growled and moved forward again. When he stopped and turned back to see if they followed, they knew something was wrong.

"Okay, Leroy. We're coming. Go get 'em, boy. We're right behind you."

CHAPTER 15

Leroy raced ahead of the truck. By the time Walker and Hannah caught up with him, he had his huge paws on the front door, demanding inside.

"Do you think it's Everett Tinker?" Hannah all but breathed the worry aloud.

"Maybe you should stay here in the truck."

Her eyes went wide with fear. "Not on your life."

"Hannah." Walker's tone was sharp.

"Two is always better than one," she reasoned. She nodded toward Leroy as he continued his ruckus. "He's scratching the door. Let's go see what's wrong."

Walker led the way, with Hannah close upon his heels. Leroy whined in appreciation as Walker reached for the handle, thanking him in dog-speak for believing. They proceeded through the first door, only to repeat the process again in the foyer. With a motion of his head for Hannah to stay behind him, Walker twisted the handle, eased open the door, and stood back as Leroy burst into the great room, ready for attack. Barking so loud the sound echoed, he made a beeline toward the little inner office, entering through the check-in desk. Before Walker and Hannah could follow, the excited white dog dashed through the opposite door, into the back hallway.

"That door was closed." Hannah put a cautioning hand on Walker's arm, her whisper urgent. "I know it was."

"Stay here. Call 9-1-1."

She shook her head. "I'm following you. And I left my phone in the truck."

Met with another door, Leroy reared up, trying to scratch his way through. Walker used the tail of his shirt to turn the knob. He tried to preserve any prints that might be on it. Leroy disappeared into the night, hot on the trail of a scent only he could detect.

"Whoever was in here is gone now," Walker reasoned.

"We should go back in. There could have been two of them."

"Maybe, but neither are in there now. Leroy would have known."

A fracas erupted somewhere near the goat pen. Startled from their sleep, the herd voiced their displeasure. Bleats and baas rent the night air.

"What is all that?" Hannah cried.

Walker turned his ear toward the racket. "I think you were right. I think there were two of them. From the sounds of it, one of them stumbled into first the goat pen, and then the chicken coop. And if that yelp and big splash I heard is any indication, I think the other one just found the creek."

A nervous giggle escaped as a mental picture popped into her head. "Oh my."

Walker shook his dark head. "That's not the word he used."

His expression was so solemn, his deadpan delivery so well done, Hannah couldn't help it. Nerves made the situation so much funnier than was warranted. Laughter burst from her chest, despite the serious situation.

To his credit, Walker tried not to laugh. A tight smile played around his lips as he concentrated on a scowl. "We should call the authorities. And we should see if anything was taken. Don't touch anything but get a visual on what they may have been doing." He dug into his pocket and pulled out his phone, punching in a number.

"You have Tracey Ann's number on speed dial?" she teased, still on a nervous high.

"Yeah. 9-1-1." As the dispatcher picked up, he spoke calmly into the phone. "This is Walker Jacoby. I'm here at the *Spirits* in Hannah, and I want to report a prowler and a possible break-in. I think there were two perpetrators, both of which are no longer on the immediate property. One may possibly be hiding in the chicken coop out back."

By the time the sheriff's department arrived, Hannah had taken stock of the situation at hand. Someone had been in the office, all right, and made a mess of it. Files were scattered all over the desk and dropped onto the floor. Pictures were off the wall and most everything was upended. The ledgers were intact but opened, every one of them scattered around the room.

"They were obviously looking for something," a young deputy stated the obvious.

"But what?" Hannah fretted.

"Lots of folks, 'specially the older ones, hide money and important papers. Tape it to the bottoms of drawers and on the backs of picture frames. Used to be a safe bet, but nowadays that's the first place a thief looks." The second deputy pointed to the ram-shackled room as case in point.

"Any other rooms disturbed?" his partner asked.

"Pictures off the walls in the great room," Hannah reported. "And you saw the check-in desk. It looks the same as this." Her sigh was weary. It would take hours to put it back into some semblance of order. Perhaps days.

"And they raided the refrigerator," Walker announced as he rejoined the group.

"Again?"

At Hannah's exasperated cry, the deputies went on alert. Deputy House, the older of the two, looked particularly concerned. "This has happened before? Say, didn't we have a call out here a few days ago? It was 10-22'd before I could get here, but wasn't it something about an intruder?"

"It... I think it was a misunderstanding," Hannah tried to explain. "There was a man."

"The one calling himself Everett Tinker?"

"No, another man. I thought he was a beggar, but then I realized he was wearing a costume. He obviously works at the history farm that is such a well-guarded secret around here. Honestly, I don't know how they expect to get—"

"Hannah," Walker broke in. There was a warning in his voice, and in the sharp look he sent her. She detected an ever-so-slight shake of his head, cautioning her to stop. *Stop her rant*, she wondered, *or the whole subject of Orlan Varela?*

"You were saying?" Deputy House prompted.

"Leroy didn't bark, so I realized he must know him. I told the dispatcher it was a mistake and made the man a sandwich." It wasn't the exact chain of events, but close.

"But you said 'again,' as if someone had raided the refrigerator before."

She shot Walker a look. "Some pork chops came up missing. I thought Walker ate them as a midnight snack."

"Wait. You two...?" This from Deputy Tedford. He wagged his finger between them, a smirk upon his face.

"No." Walker's barked denial was sharp enough to sting. It bit right into Hannah's pride, as he went on to explain, "Miss Duncan is my client. She's new to the area, and to the country lifestyle, in fact, having lived in Houston most of her life. To put her at ease, I have been staying here at the inn until the Tanners return from their cruise."

The lawman broke into a guffaw. "I bet old Fred and Sadie are having the time of their lives! I can just imagine Fred out there on the water!"

Irritated at both men, Hannah's voice was sardonic. "Can we get back to the case, please? Aren't you going to take fingerprints, test for DNA, anything?"

"This isn't Houston, miss, and it sure ain't CSI," Deputy House drawled. "Things don't work in real life like they do on TV, and small departments don't work like they do in big cities. We can't. We don't have the funding."

"So, no fingerprints?"

"We could," he agreed, but his tone was dubious. "But the dust makes an awful mess. Might leave a smudge on all those papers, and some of those ledgers look pretty old. You sure you want to do that?"

Hannah looked around the room. She hated the thought of ruining all those old ledgers, particularly when she hadn't gone through all of them yet. Plus, she thoroughly enjoyed the side notes. As it turned out, Miss Wilhelmina carried on a habit started back in the early ledgers, when the inn was still a stagecoach stop. Those books had true historical value. Hannah couldn't bear the thought of ruining them with black powder.

"I guess not," she said, looking to Walker for confirmation. He lifted one shoulder, signaling that the choice was hers. "Maybe just the door handles."

"Good call," House nodded his approval. "Ted, go get the kit. I'll finish up pictures of this mess."

Hannah made her way toward Walker. From the side of her mouth, she hissed, "We need to talk."

CHAPTER 16

Back at the motel, the brothers cleaned up after their disastrous mission.

"I can't believe I have chicken feathers in my nostrils!" Delroy whined, still digging for more.

"At least you didn't have to ride home soaking wet," his brother complained. He sloshed across the carpet, leaving a wet path to the bathroom. "Turned my ankle when I fell down the hill and into that creek, don't you know."

"At least you didn't meet up on the wrong end of an angry goat."

"Goat? I thought you were roosting with the chickens."

"I stumbled into the goat pen first. There was a fence between us, but that didn't stop a mean billy from letting me know I weren't welcome." Delroy rubbed at the offended area.

"So, how'd you end up wearing feathers?" Bigs dropped his overalls to the floor, unconcerned that his saggy underwear was now on display.

"Cover that thing!" his brother protested. "The only way to get away from that shaggy monster of a dog was to let myself into the chicken coop. Thought he would tear the pen down, I did, until that lawyer guy called him back to the house. As soon as I could, I skedaddled outta there."

"And all for nothing. We didn't find a dad-blamed thing, don't you know." Bigs shook his head in disgust. "I'm taking a hot shower."

"Leave some hot water for me this time!" Delroy said to the slamming door.

Delroy dusted off the last of the feathers. Bigs claimed the curse against his family was broken, but he had his doubts. Same as always, nothing was going their way.

His entire life, the Hatfield family had been down on their luck. No matter what happened, they never seemed to catch a break. There were no doctors or lawyers in their family tree; hardly a high school diploma, if the truth be known. He wondered if his was the sole exception. Bigs had a GED certificate, but it had come in the mail through one of those back-of-the-magazine offers. Send a few bucks, answer a few questions, and your 'diploma' arrived in the mail in six to twelve weeks. Most of the other men in their family dropped out of school to enter the workforce. Day laborers, every one of them. Not that there was a single thing wrong with an honest day's work for honest wages. For the Hatfield family, though, the problem came when one tried to define the word 'honest.' It wasn't a common word in their vocabulary.

His father, and Big Daddy before him, and his father before him, always blamed it on the curse. Said the old Indian woman had put a hex on Patch's head all those years ago, at the request of Lina Hannah. Said for all the days of their lives, their descendants would be bound by the curse. Bigs claimed that with the death of Wilhelmina Hannah (the last descendant of the cursor), the hex was broken for the descendants of the cursee (which was them.)

When his older brother said it, it sounded a lot more convincing. When Del ran the words through his own head, especially when wearing these dad-burned feathers, it just sounded like wishful thinking.

CHAPTER 17

"So, what's so urgent we have to talk about?" Walker asked. Hannah had shuffled him out of the office, all but pushing him across the hall and into the kitchen.

"Why didn't you want me mentioning Orlan Varela? He could be working with Everett Tinker as an inside man!"

"Believe me, Hannah. Orlan Varela isn't working with Tinker."

"How do you know that? Someone stole those pork chops, and that man was definitely standing here in the kitchen a few days ago, going on about how good it smelled in here." She jerked open the refrigerator door and peered inside. "Oh, and now someone has gone and eaten the pizza from last night, and the stew from the night before. They even stole the plastic container it was in!"

"I'll buy you some more Tupperware," he promised. "But take my advice. Don't mention Orlan Varela's name to the deputies."

"And why not? Is he someone important?" Her eyes narrowed in suspicion. "Is he the sheriff's son or something? The county judge's nephew? Is there a reason they wouldn't want to know he might be involved in this?"

"He wasn't involved," Walker insisted stubbornly.

"You can't know that!"

"I can."

"Just like you know Caroline wasn't involved." She sneered, crossing her arms over her chest. "Wait. Are they your clients? Is that why you're trying to protect them?"

"Hardly," he snorted.

"Then explain to me why I shouldn't march over there and ask Deputy House to look into this evening's whereabouts of Orlan Varela?"

"You don't need House for that," House's partner said, walking in to hear the end of her rant. "I can answer that question for you. Same place he is every night, just down the road. Buried in the Grapetown Cemetery."

"Buried? But, how—oh, I get it. He's someone famous from the *past*. Okay, so maybe you can find out who plays his character at the history farm."

The deputy sent Walker a curious look, before directing his scowl at Hannah. "Ma'am, where is this history farm you keep talking about?"

"How should I know? I can't find a thing about it on the internet. But you're from here, you should know!"

"I have no idea what you're talking about."

Hannah looked at Walker for support. "You tell him. Tell him how Caroline works there, just like the man who was in this kitchen."

"I think I heard House calling you," Walker lied to the deputy. "Hannah, can I have a word?"

Both looked confused, but both complied. Tedford left the kitchen and Hannah came forward, wearing a frown. "Would you please tell me what's going on?"

When Walker's hand went to the back of his neck, she knew it wouldn't be good.

"Like I said, there's something I've been meaning to tell you. About Caroline..." he started. "And Varela. The thing is..."

Hannah felt a chill move down her back. Behind her, someone spoke.

"What the gentleman is trying to say," a familiar honeyed voice purred with its heavy Southern drawl, "is that the good officers of the law don't know we're here."

Hannah whirled around to face the elusive Caroline. She looked every bit as lovely as she had the other day, dressed again in her yellow hoop skirts. Once again, Hannah was conscious of her own less-than-elegant appearance, which was now dusted quite generously with sand.

"Where did you come from? How do you keep getting in here?"

The delicate blonde looked at Walker. "She doesn't know, does she, Barrister Jacoby?"

He shook his head.

Hannah resented the fact the two of them shared a secret and left her out. "I don't know what?" she snapped. "That you're involved? It's becoming rather obvious!"

"Involved?" The woman looked truly confused.

"You know. The two of you." She waved her hand suggestively, but the blonde still looked clueless. Hannah rolled her eyes. "Dating. Having an affair. Hooking up. Whatever it is you choose to call it."

"Hannah, you're way off base," Walker tried to tell her.

She shook her hair. Bits of sand fell from her dark locks, a side effect from her earlier tumble. "I don't think so, although I am questioning your judgment right about now," Hannah said shortly. Caroline still had a blank look upon her lovely face.

As her meaning finally sank in, Caroline flushed a deep, angry red, truly offended. "Well, I never!" she huffed. "How dare you, madam? How dare you insinuate such a vile thing against my character?"

"Hey, it turns out he's not married after all, so he's unattached."

"But I, madam, am not," the blonde sniffed indignantly. "I am betrothed to my beloved, Captain Ezekiel Musebach of Company A, Gillespie Rifles, of the Third Texas Infantry. I would never besmirch his good name, particularly at a time when he risks his very life, fighting in this dreadful War Between the States."

It was Hannah's turn to adopt a blank stare. The woman spoke with very precise dialect, heavily flavored with a Southern accent. If Hannah had questioned the woman's mental stability before, there was no longer any doubt. She definitely had problems. The woman thought she was engaged to a Confederate soldier who still fought in the war.

"What Caroline is trying to say is that—"

Before Walker could continue, Deputy Tedford returned. "False alarm," he said. "If you'll excuse me, I'll dust for prints here on the refrigerator. Anywhere else you think he touched?"

Hannah looked from the officer to Caroline, and back again. He hadn't acknowledged the newcomer to his investigation.

"Do you not notice anything different from a few moments ago?" Hannah couldn't resist asking.

The officer looked around, his brow buckled with concentration. His eyes zeroed in on a spot just beside Caroline's feet. Her dainty black boots peeked out from beneath frilly ruffled petticoats and the wide bell of her skirt.

"I see it now," he said, striding forward.

Hannah sighed in relief. At least the officer wasn't as inept as she was beginning to fear. But why was he advancing toward the woman with such determination? Did he think she was dangerous? Did he plan to take her into custody?

Hannah might have worried about it, but the oddest thing happened next. Deputy Tedford walked right up to the woman, well past what was considered the appropriate bounds. He bent down, intent on retrieving the spoon he saw on the floor. The spoon whose handle Caroline appeared to be standing upon. Without a word, he bent to scoop it up. As he did, the impossible happened: his head went through—*through!*—the yellow hoop dress.

Caroline never moved. Never squealed. Never disparaged the officer for so rudely intruding into her personal space and ruffling her skirt. After the tongue lashing she gave Hannah for insulting her character, such an insult upon her person would surely be far worse. Yet the woman never moved. Her *skirt* never moved, even though Hannah had seen the officer's head move right into the fabric.

Hannah felt dizzy. Something wasn't right. The officer paused, turning back toward them, halfway into the task. The movement pushed his shoulders into Caroline's body, yet she remained perfectly still.

"You drop this or did the perp?" he asked. He was completely unconcerned about the woman he all but shoved to the floor. Unconcerned with the yellow fabric that shrouded his face. Unconcerned with the expression of utter disbelief upon Hannah's face.

Hannah still didn't understand. She could see him perfectly through the yellow haze. His shoulder was about where Caroline's thigh should be. His face was dangerously close to her most intimate areas. Why hadn't the hoops pushed him away? Why hadn't Caroline?

As if reading her thoughts, Caroline lifted her hand and slapped the officer, right across the top of his head. Her hand never touched him. In fact, it passed *through* the officer's head. He never felt a thing.

Because there's nothing to feel.

The knowledge hit Hannah with staggering force.

Caroline is a ghost!

Walker watched the realization play out across her face. She was pale, as pale now as Caroline. "Hannah?" he asked in concern. "Do you need to sit down?"

She opened her mouth to speak, but no sound came out. "Yes," she finally squeaked. Then she shook her head. "No. No, I think I need to lie down. I need to go to my room. Now!" Her voice took on a note of urgency.

Panic, was more like it. This couldn't be happening!

And yet, it was. Caroline, the ghost, took several steps forward, passing completely through the officer. Just as her image crossed over him, he stood. For a moment in time, their bodies intertwined, a man's khaki uniform blending into a woman's fancy yellow dress. His head appeared to sit atop hers. Had it not been so startling, the image might have been funny.

Hannah wasn't laughing. Hannah was considering being sick, right there on the kitchen floor.

She had to get out of here, and she had to get out now.

"Hannah?"

Walker raced after her, following her up the stairs two at a time. Hannah had no idea how she had gotten up the stairs so quickly, but she was already opening the door to her suite when his boot hit the landing.

"Hannah, are you okay?"

She turned to him, her face blanched with shock and her lips trembling. "No, Walker. No, I am not okay. Hank Ruby was murdered. Someone trashed my office tonight, most likely his killer. My house was broken into. But that's not even the strangest part. The strangest part is that I now live here, in this house. With a ghost. A ghost, Walker. A walking, talking ghost. A ghost!" Her voice rose to a trill with her last words. She opened the door and rushed inside, flinging herself across the bed.

Walker caught the door before it slammed in his face. He stood quietly for a long moment, allowing her time to gather her thoughts. He finally took a seat beside her prone body.

"I know this must be a shock," he started. His tone was apologetic.

"It shouldn't be," she realized. "So many things didn't add up, didn't make sense." She played through them in her mind. "I just never dreamed..."

"And why would you? This is completely outside the norm."

"Caroline is one of the 'special guests' I must continue to accommodate, isn't she?" Hannah asked quietly.

"Yes."

"So, there must be others."

Walker appreciated her quick mind. Most of all, he appreciated her acceptance. This could have been so much more difficult, if she hadn't been a believer. "Two others, that I am aware of. Orlan Varela is one of them."

"Of course he is." It made sense now. "The other?"

The lawyer looked slightly uncomfortable. He did that thing, scrubbing at his neck again. "An old Indian medicine woman. We think her name is Gouyen, which means wise woman. She rarely appears, and when she does, she has little to say."

"Okay, from the look on your face, I don't think I can handle that one right now," Hannah decided. "Tell me about Caroline." Despite her earlier assessment of the woman, she seemed the least harmful of them.

To her surprise, Walker scooted further onto the bed and stretched out beside her. They both lay on their backs, staring up at the ceiling.

"Her name is Caroline Hamilton, and she is—was—the daughter of a wealthy landowner. They came from Georgia, just before the Civil War started. Her father married a German widow who owned several leagues of land. Apparently, they had a home nearby."

"Who's this Bo she's engaged to? And why did she later call him by another name?"

Walker chuckled at her blunder. "Not Bo, b-o. Beau, as in the old-fashioned name for a boyfriend. Her *intended*, as she calls him. He was a local man who signed up to fight in the war. From what we can tell, he was killed in the war and never came home."

"That's terrible. No wonder she's still searching for him!"

"They say she was never quite right after that. One night, she wandered out of the house and into the woods. They found her the next morning, in the creek out back."

Hannah visibly recoiled. "That's so tragic!" Her voice was filled with sorrow.

Walker shrugged. "It was a hundred and fifty-odd years ago."

"But she's still... here."

"Miss Wilhelmina said she can't cross over, until she knows for certain what happened to her fiancé."

"But she may never know."

"Exactly."

Hannah's hand moved outward, within a hair's breadth of his. For some reason, she felt the need for human contact right now.

"And Orlan?"

"Orlan is a local unsung hero. Way back when this was still a stage stop, sometime around 1877 or 78, there was a big stagecoach robbery not far from here. Legend has it that a huge shipment of gold was on the stage, en route to—"

"I know this story!" Enthusiasm colored her voice. She tapped his hand in excitement. "I just read about it!"

He caught her fingers to still them. "So, you probably know about Lina Hannah, Ezekiel Hannah's youngest daughter. Her father said he was too busy to care for the injured man, so she took it upon herself to nurse him back to health. Supposedly, they fell in love while he was recuperating. The problem was that Orlan, a local cowboy who had known Lina for most of her life, was also in love with her. He told her the man with the patched eye was trouble, but Lina didn't believe him. She loved him anyway."

"A patch? I don't think I read about that."

"Apparently, he was a rough-looking hombre, with a patch over one eye and a scar on his cheek."

"I saw his wanted poster! It's hanging in the saloon!" Her fingers danced again, so Walker held them tight within his own.

"Anyway, come to find out, the man was one of the ones who robbed the stage. For a while, they said it was a one-man job, but later, they found out that the infamous Sam Bass and his gang were also in on it. Legend has it they hid the gold and were all killed before they could come back for it. Everyone except the man with the patch. Lina saw a letter meant for her father, alerting him that he harbored a dangerous criminal. Before they could arrest them, Lina persuaded Orlan to help the man escape."

Hannah frowned. "Where's the part where he's a hero? He helped an outlaw get away."

"Maybe, maybe not. Lina insisted it was all a mistake, that the men on the stage only *thought* her man was trying to rob it. According to him, he was tired of Texas and was going back to Kansas. He just wanted to bum a ride on the stage. But that's beside the point. The point is, Orlan helped the man escape, but he made him promise to leave Texas and never come back. In turn, Orlan vowed to watch over Lina and to protect her with his life, which is exactly what he did."

"What happened?"

"Word of the hidden gold got out. What's more, rumor was that the outlaw left a map of how to find it, here at the stage stop. More than one greedy soul tried to barge their way in and find the map. Tore up the inn looking for it, on more than one occasion, so they say."

Hannah's sigh was heavy with empathy. "I know the feeling. Just like what happened here tonight."

"Two of the men to come here took their anger and greed out on Lina. They accused her of knowing where the treasure was and of helping the outlaw escape. They would have done her great harm, possibly killed her, if Orlan hadn't arrived when he did. He killed the men, saved Lina, but suffered a mortal wound. After refusing him for years, Lina finally married him on his deathbed, just before he took his final breath."

Hannah gave him a reproachful look. "Has anyone ever told you that you're a terrible storyteller? You only know sad tales!"

"You asked me about the ghosts, Hannah. They aren't ghosts, unless they die."

"But their stories are both so tragic and sad!"

"Probably the reason they can't cross over," he reasoned. "Unfinished business here on earth, and all that."

"I suppose Orlan stayed behind to watch over Lina?"

"It looks that way."

"But she's long dead by now, and apparently he's still here."

"Something about vowing to protect all that was hers and carrying out the curse."

Hannah stiffened. "What curse?"

Walker waved a dismissive hand, the one not holding hers. "Something about the old Indian woman and a curse she put on the descendants of the outlaw's family. The one-eyed man broke Lina's heart, so she put a hex on him, or something to that order. I don't really believe in hexing, to tell you the truth."

"Yet you believe in ghosts."

When he shrugged his broad shoulders, the movement echoed across the mattress where they lay. "It's hard not to, when you see them every day."

Hannah was silent, trying to absorb all that he told her. It was a lot to deal with.

"Is this the reason for the thirty-day stipulation?" she asked after a while.

"Yes. Miss Wilhelmina wanted to know that the person who took her place would be strong enough, and brave enough, to stay, knowing there were ghosts on the property. She didn't want a non-believer taking over."

"I guess the imprisonment clause was to make sure the ghosts appeared during that time?" she guessed.

She heard the frown, even though she couldn't see it while staring at the ceiling. "It's not an imprisonment, Hannah. But yes, that was the general idea. To be honest, I'm surprised they presented themselves to you so early. I thought for sure it would take them another week or so."

"So now what?"

"So now you tell me about your plans for the inn."

"You didn't seem too interested in them earlier this evening." His rejection still stung.

"Only because you didn't know about the ghosts. I had no idea how you would react and if you would even want to stay, once you knew the truth."

Hannah considered his words for a long moment.

She still knew nothing about running an inn.

Her life, and her friends, were in Houston. When he wasn't traveling the globe, so was JoeJoe.

But that phase of her life was over. Her friends were busy with new lives of their own. JoeJoe would always be her uncle, no matter where she lived. No matter what crazy gift he gave her next.

It was time for a new career, a new challenge, and this one seemed interesting. It was definitely challenging. She wasn't a country girl, and yet it had already gotten into her blood.

It wasn't without downfalls.

For one thing, she could be in serious danger. Someone— probably the same person who killed Hank Ruby—had broken into the inn, searching for some unknown object. For another, there were ghosts here.

Yet for the first time in a very long time, Hannah felt a stir of excitement in her blood.

It could have something to do with the man lying beside her. There was no denying the attraction between them, even though she had to ignore it. Married or not, Walker Jacoby was off limits.

Most likely, it had to do with the feeling of accomplishment seeping into her soul. She felt an enormous sense of pride just this morning, over something as simple as milking a cow.

This was something she could do on her own. Without her family's help. Okay, so JoeJoe played a huge part in acquiring the town, but only the purchase. The rest she had done on her own.

Did she want to stay, danger, ghosts, and all?

"I do," she realized quietly. Her voice took on new strength. "In spite of it all, and as crazy as it seems, I want to stay."

CHAPTER 18

After making a few early morning calls, Walker cleared his schedule for the day. Hannah wouldn't admit it, but she was secretly glad to have him there. Events from the previous evening left her more shaken than she cared to admit.

It was bad enough knowing she lived among ghosts. In her mind, however, it was much worse, living with the fear of prowlers. Even in the broad light of day, she felt vulnerable.

They tended the animals before tackling the ransacked inn. Walker worked the check-in area, while Hannah tried to bring order to her office. Despite an hour's work, the rooms were still disasters. At the rate they were going, the Tanners would arrive home to a huge mess.

"I wonder what they were looking for," she mused aloud, stooping to gather up a handful of scattered ledgers. Other than an added scuff here or there, or a crumpled page or two, none seemed any worse for the experience.

"Could be anything. Cash, credit card numbers, the address of previous guests... anything."

"And why would someone want a previous guest's address?" Hannah scoffed.

Walker's voice floated through the open doorway. She could practically hear the shrug in his words. "There are all kinds of scams these days. Who knows what nefarious deed someone may be cooking up next?"

"Or," Hannah suggested sweetly, straightening a picture on the wall that separated them, "it could be something less malicious. Maybe Everett Tinker fell in love with a guest last summer, and he's trying to find the person's address, so he can rekindle the romance."

She heard his doubtful grunt. "In that case, it would be more likely so he could stalk her. This isn't the work of a love-sick fool."

"You have a point," she conceded. "I can picture him the sick fool, but not a *love*-sick fool."

"We have to keep an open mind, you know. Everett Tinker may have nothing to do with this. No matter how much we both dislike the man, he is innocent until proven guilty, you know."

She gave an ungracious grunt. "Spoken like a true lawyer."

"Is that an insult?" he challenged, popping his dark head around the doorway.

"Take it how you may. My money is on Tinker, or whatever his name is." She propped her hands onto her hips and added saucily, "Don't you know."

Walker stepped into the room, holding a framed painting. One look told Hannah that it was very old.

"I'm glad these all survived. Lina Hannah painted these, you know, almost a century ago."

"You're kidding!"

"Actually, she was very talented. These were done when she was in her later years, but even the ones she did as a teen-ager were good. She loved color, as you can see in the painting." He flashed a rueful smile. "And in half the furnishings."

"Furnishings?"

"Haven't you noticed how many of the older pieces are painted? My room has one blue chest, and one yellow one. The colors have faded over the years, but once upon a time, I imagine they were rather bright."

"I noticed there was an old green chest in my room. It has some sort of decorative border around it."

"Lina's handiwork, no doubt."

"That's amazing," Hannah said. "That would make it over a hundred years old."

"One thing's for certain. They don't make furniture like they used to." Walker carried the picture back to its place on the other side of the wall. After a few moments, he returned. "When the Tanners get in and settled, I have some errands I need to run. While I'm out, I thought I'd drive by the motels in Fredericksburg, and see if I spot Tinker's truck in any of the parking lots."

"Good idea. But at least Fred will be here then," she added, batting her eyes and slipping into a Southern accent similar to

Caroline's. "You know, to protect us poor, helpless females." She fanned herself with the sheaf of papers in her hand. "We shall have the protection of at least one brave gentleman to guard our honor and protect us from that evil Yankee."

Not only did Walker look amused, he also looked a bit confused. Before Hannah could whiz him on his response, Leroy lumbered to his feet and barked with excitement. His wagging tail knocked over a stack of papers Hannah had recently righted.

"Leroy, look what you did!" she wailed in frustration. She squatted down to collect the papers. Again.

"Judging from his bark, I think Fred and Sadie have arrived," Walker predicted. "Is that it, boy? Have your people come home?"

"They're going to think I'm the worse housekeeper ever! Just look at this mess!"

Walker was nonplussed. "Just wait until they get a hold of these rooms. They'll have them back in shape in no time." He offered his hand in help. "Shall we go greet them?"

Deciding there was no way she could have the room in order by the time the couple walked inside, she admitted defeat and placed her hand in his. He kept hold of it as he helped her maneuver the cluttered pathway, and even as they found their way into the front room. He dropped her hand as he opened the door, but Hannah wanted to think the hand on her back was his way of showing his support when he introduced her to the other couple.

What should she call them, she wondered idly, as she pushed through the dual doors. Mr. and Mrs.? Or should she keep it informal, and call them Sadie and Fred? Technically, she was now their employer.

A gleaming red 1953 Cadillac LeMans, fully restored and in excellent condition, claimed residency outside the old stage-coach stop. Leroy's paws rested on the closed roof of the convertible, as he attempted to stuff his furry head inside the partially opened window. From inside the passenger's side, a person laughed at the dog's exuberance.

The driver's door opened, and a petite woman stepped out. Despite being seventy if she were a day, she wore a complete western get-up on her tiny frame: starched denim Wrangler jeans, a black shirt with white western-style piping and shiny pearl snaps, a thin ostrich-skin belt with an oversized heart-shaped buckle, and red-tooled cowboy boots. With fringe. Perched atop her carefully arranged gray curls, a matching red-felt cowboy hat rested.

Just for a moment, Hannah wondered if this were another ghost. Annie Oakley, perhaps?

"Leroy!" the little woman called with glee. "We're home, boy!"

Getting a glimpse of his mistress, the beast abandoned the window and lunged over the top of the car toward her. Instead of scolding him for scratching the paint, Hannah watched as the woman, obviously Sadie, laughed with joy and greeted the huge dog in an equally big bear hug. *Or is it a dog hug?* A hug that consisted of fur, at any rate.

"Well, I see how I rate!" a voice boomed from the passenger side. The door opened, and another woman stepped from the vehicle, shaking her gray head in amusement. She was only slightly taller than the first woman, but thicker made. Her casual Hawaiian shirt and Bermuda shorts were at complete odds with her companion's sharp, neat appearance.

"Welcome home!" As Walker greeted the two women with hugs, his voice warmed with true affection. Hannah was so bemused with the scene before her—a flurry of elbows and cheeks turned every which way, and all managing over the dancing, prancing, happily squirming giant of a dog—that she failed to immediately notice they were missing a major player. *Where*, she finally thought to wonder, *is Fred Tanner?*

After a second round of hugs and plenty of laughter, Walker succeeded in turning the ladies' attention to Hannah, who stood by, patiently waiting with a smile.

"Oh, my heavens, what a lovely young woman!" This, from the woman wearing the colorful shirt. She slapped both hands to her own face and beamed happily at Hannah. "I never dreamed our new owner would be so young! Sister, have you ever seen such gorgeous hair in all your life? Just look at that thick mane! And, oh, those blue eyes! Why, she's just a living doll!"

"Just what we need around here," the second woman agreed with a vigorous nod. "Fresh, young blood! With new ideas to stir a little life into these dusty old buildings. Oh, what a sight for sore eyes you are! Wilhelmina would be so proud."

Walker made the introductions with a flourish. "Ladies, may I present to you the new owner of your fair town and, in fact, your employer, Hannah Duncan. Hannah, it is my pleasure to introduce you to the Tanner sisters, Sadie and Fredrika. Or as we all know her, Fred."

Holy boomtown! Fred Tanner is a woman!

How had she not known this? In all their conversations, gender had never come up, so she had simply assumed... Hannah's mouth hung open for a full moment, before she gathered her senses enough to snap it shut.

"It's a pleasure to meet you!" The woman in the cowgirl outfit pulled a stunned Hannah into a warm embrace.

Hannah was confused now—was this Sadie, or Fred?—but she returned the friendly gesture.

"Don't hog the girl all to yourself, Fred!" the other woman chided. "Let me hug her, too."

"Oh, there's plenty of room for a group hug, Sadie Jean. Get on over here and see for yourself."

Hannah found herself sandwiched between the two sisters and their warm, welcoming hug. Unaccustomed to such a greeting, Hannah found it oddly touching, if not a bit overwhelming. She waited what she hoped was an acceptable time before pulling away.

"I'm so happy you're back," she told them. "How was your trip?"

The innocent question launched a barrage of animated conversation, as both sisters spoke at once. Hannah tried to keep up, swiveling her head back and forth as she listened to first one woman, and then the other. When Sadie launched into a detailed description of the sumptuous buffets on board the ship and her sister started a review of the shows they had seen, Walker stepped up and tactfully herded Fred aside. Hannah flashed him a grateful smile. He had surely saved her from a definite case of whiplash.

A full ten minutes later, the sisters finally ran out of steam. "Whew! That plumb tuckered me out, just telling about it," Sadie decided. "Sister, let's go inside and make sure things are all tidied up for our guest." She turned to beam at Hannah. "We have the most delightful surprise for you."

Before she could tell her what it was, her sister broke in, "You have your very first guest arriving!" Fred blurted out.

Both sisters beamed and nodded in tandem, clearly proud to be the bearers of such wonderful news.

Hannah's reaction wasn't what they expected. "Guest?" she cried in dismay. "What are you talking about?"

Sadie patted her arm. "You can thank us later, dear. It was the most wonderful coincidence. We stopped in town to pick up milk and bread—"

"—and to give Clara Schmidt the Mexican vanilla we picked up for her in Cancun—"

"That, too," Sadie agreed, unconcerned with how her sister kept butting into her sentences. "And we just happened to bump into the nicest gentleman. He was looking for a place to stay, and, what with the festival this week, town is hopping like a June bug on a summer bonfire. He couldn't find a decent hotel room—"

"—for just one night. Everyone insisted on a two to three night minimum. Can you imagine?" Fred shook her head with a tsk-tsk.

"So, naturally, Sister and I told him he could book a single night here. It won't be any bother, now that we're back."

"We'll put the room to order, before we even unpack our suitcases," Fred promised. "And in the morning—"

"—I'll make him a breakfast fit for a king!" Sadie clapped her hands together, as if the matter were settled.

"But you don't understand. The inn isn't ready for guests yet," Hannah protested.

"It's just one man, for one night," Sadie said.

"Think of it as a trial run. A chance to get your feet wet, before you jump head first into a cold creek!" Fred added with a bright smile.

"No, you don't understand. We can't accommodate guests yet. The place is a disaster!"

"Now, now," Sadie said, patting Hannah's arm again. "Don't fret your pretty little head about it. Not everyone's as tidy a housekeeper as Fred. You just wait. Give us an hour, and we'll have everything right as rain."

Hannah threw Walker a beseeching look. When Sadie would have marched up to the front porch of the old inn, the lawyer stepped in her way.

"What Miss Duncan is trying to tell you," he asserted, his voice firm, "is that we had an intruder last night. He made quite a mess of both offices. The place truly is a disaster."

"An intruder!"

"Was anything stolen?"

Fred clasped her hand to her heart. "They didn't steal the good silver, did they?"

Good silver? Hannah hadn't noticed any good silver.

"From what we can tell, nothing was stolen," Walker assured the women. "But we're still putting things to rights."

"The ledgers are okay, aren't they?" Sadie looked worried.

Hannah understood her concerns and nodded. "Yes, they appear to be. I've been reading through them the last few days, so they were one of the first things I checked. A few wrinkled pages, but nothing too damaged."

"Oh, thank the dear Lord. Those ledgers hold the history of the inn, you know."

"Yes," Hannah agreed with a smile. "I've enjoyed reading the notes jotted down here and there. It's almost like a journal."

Her answer pleased Sadie. With a wink to her sister, the gray-haired woman cooed, "Ooh, we've got ourselves a keeper, Fred. She's going to fit in here just fine."

"In more ways than you can imagine," Walker agreed with an enigmatic smile. He opened the door and gave a gallant sweep of his arm. "Ladies, after you."

CHAPTER 19

True to their word, Fred and Sadie swept into the inn like twin cyclones. While Sadie whipped the front office into a semblance of order, Fred tackled Room 3.

Before Hannah could finish sweeping the front room and straightening the chairs, Fred came bounding down the stairs with a satisfied smile upon her face.

"All done," she reported. "The Houston Room is ready for our guest."

Hannah frowned. "Which one is the Houston Room? I didn't realize they had names."

Fred lifted a delicate shoulder. "Wilhelmina and I were great friends, but that is one thing we disagreed on. I thought the rooms should have their own identities. You may have noticed, they each have their own decor. Their own personality, if you will."

Personality, Hannah wondered, *or ghost?*

"So which room is the Houston Room?"

"Room 3, just like we discussed."

"We also discussed canceling the booking, yet you still changed the linens."

"Of course I did. Those things were all dusty from no use." She waved her hand in dismissal. "And of course, we couldn't cancel the booking. We didn't get a telephone number."

"But—" Hannah bit back her protest. From the look on Fred's face, it would do no good to argue.

And here I thought I was the boss, Hannah groused, with an imagined roll of her eyes. *Clearly, these ladies run things around here.*

If she were being honest, it was probably a good thing. Hannah didn't know the first thing about running an inn.

"Don't worry, by the time he checks in, you'll never know anything was amiss last night."

Hannah looked doubtful, but Fred's smile was confident.

Sadie poked her gray head out from the check-in cubicle. "All done in here!" she called merrily. "If it's okay with you, we'll dash up to the house, unpack, and be back before our guest arrives. I wouldn't look for him until after dinner. We told him the kitchen was closed this evening."

Her comment brought up a new worry. "Oh, that's right," Hannah fretted. "You mentioned breakfast. I'm not sure we have the makings for it."

Both women were instantly alarmed. "You didn't get rid of the girls, did you?" Sadie's voice rose with a touch of hysteria. "Henny Penny and Loosey Goosey? They're our best laying hens!"

"Please tell me Buttercrunch is still here." Fred's lower lip trembled with worry.

"Of course, of course," Hannah was quick to assure the sisters. "All of the animals are still here, right down to the chickens. Nothing has changed."

"Oh, thank the good Lord," Sadie said in relief. "You had me scared there for a minute. As long as we have eggs, milk, and flour, we have the makings for breakfast."

"It's just that... I didn't plan for extra people." Did they know about the imprisonment clause? She wasn't exactly free to run to the grocery store and pick up last-minute supplies.

"Walker is in town right now," Sadie pointed out. "I'll check out the kitchen, make a list, and have him pick up anything else I need." She started toward the hallway but stopped herself. Glancing worriedly at Hannah, she said with a cloud of uncertainty, "That is, if you want me to continue doing the cooking. I suppose with you being the new owner and all, you might be making some changes."

Torn between needing to assert her authority and wanting to reassure the older woman, Hannah tried to accomplish both. "For now, I see no reason to change things. I would appreciate you preparing breakfast for our guests." She shot the other sister a smile, as well. "And thank you, Fred, for preparing the room. Now, if one of you would be so kind as to show me how to get into the computer..."

"Come with me," said Fred, crooking her slender finger.

With the Tanner sisters gone, the inn seemed particularly quiet. Walker was still in town, Leroy had followed the red Cadillac to the cabin in the woods, and there was no sign of Orlan Varela or Caroline today. Hannah was alone at the inn.

She kept the doors locked as she worked in the front office. Before leaving, Fred gave her a quick tutorial on how the reservation system worked, jotted down the passwords to various programs, and left Hannah to poke through the computer at her own pace.

Caught up in teaching herself how everything worked, Hannah was soon oblivious to time, but the sound of an approaching car finally snagged her attention. A glance at the clock confirmed she had been hunched over the computer for most of the afternoon.

The vehicle didn't sound like Walker's truck, but perhaps it was Fred and Sadie. Hannah finger-combed her long tresses as she hurried to the front door.

A hint of worry niggled its way up her spine. Instead of the vintage convertible she expected, she saw a nondescript dark sedan. Had their first guest already arrived?

Apparently so. A man stepped from the backseat with a duffel bag in his hand. He spoke to the driver and then stood back so the car could pull away. Rather than move forward, he stood for a long moment, looking over the property. Something in his sweeping gaze made Hannah increasingly uncomfortable. *Where*, she wondered, *was everyone?* Walker should have been back by now, and the Tanner sisters hadn't returned yet, either. That meant she was here alone with a man who eyed the place as if it were a side of prime beef.

She thought of Everett Tinker, and how he had ogled the property in much the same manner. Thank the Lord, this man looked nothing like the obnoxious handyman. This man was much smaller, almost thin. Even though his jeans and t-shirt were faded and a bit worn, they looked clean and fit him better than the baggy overalls of the carpenter.

"Stop it," Hannah hissed to herself. "This isn't Everett Tinker. This man has a reservation. He's just looking over the place, wondering if he made a wise choice. Perfectly normal, under the circumstances." She gave a rueful snort and muttered, "Lord knows, it doesn't look like much."

No need adding to his discomfort by looking too eager. Hannah unlocked the door and hurried back to her cubicle. She grabbed her phone and saw she missed a text from Walker, saying he stopped at the office and would be later than expected. *Great*, she moaned. And somehow, she had failed to get a number for the Tanners. It really was just her, and the man now coming through the door.

Hannah gathered her courage and tried to sound more congenial than she felt. "Hello," she called, "and welcome to *The Spirits of Texas Inn*." She hoped her forced smile didn't waver.

The man glanced around the big open room, blinking in rapid succession. Hannah felt a stab of empathy for him. He was obviously nervous, wondering what he had gotten himself into.

"Excuse the mess," Hannah said, her voice now warmed with sincerity. "We're under new management and haven't had time to sort everything out yet. I apologize for the current state." In truth, the room looked exactly as it had when she first arrived. With no visible signs of last night's break-in, her apology was directed more to the drab interior and the outdated furnishings.

"Looks better than I expected," the man remarked, moving forward.

Hannah tried not to frown. She wasn't certain, but the statement could have been an insult. Then again, she reasoned, it may have been a backhanded compliment. Either way, she suspected it was truth. Given the bedraggled appearance of the town as a whole, it didn't inspire high expectations.

Interjecting a note of brightness into her voice, Hannah tried another smile. "Do you have a reservation?"

"Yeah, sort of. I met a couple of women in town who said I should stay here. One of 'em was dressed in a cowgirl get-up, and the other one was in a Hawaiian shirt with big flowers all over it." His hand twirled in the air, indicating the pattern of bold flowers Sadie had worn. "They said they could set me up for the night."

"Certainly. I'll just need to see your driver's license and credit card, please. If you'll fill out this form, we'll get you right into a room." Hannah smiled and pushed the clipboard toward him.

Instead of reaching for the paper, the man scratched his head and gnawed on his lower lip. "Yeah, well, about that..."

Alarms went off in Hannah's head as her smile slipped. "Is there a problem?"

"Well, you see, I don't exactly have a driver's license. And my ole pappy taught me to pay cash wherever I go. 'Son,' he always said, 'a man can get in a heap 'o trouble, charging and owing his whole life. Pay cash, and you never got ta worry.'" He left out part of what his father taught him, the part about not leaving a trail. Cash was the preferred method when you wanted to stay incognito.

"I'm sorry, but without proper means of identification, I'm afraid we can't give you a room."

Hannah heard herself saying the words, even as she wondered where they came from. They simply flowed from her mouth, as if she had been formally trained for the job. *Common sense*, she assured herself. She had stayed at enough hotels to know the drill. Hadn't everyone?

"That's why I had the car drop me off, you see. It's one of those newfangled taxis, where you call up a number and they send someone to pick you up in their own car. Being as I don't have a license, I can't rightly drive a vehicle. Wouldn't want to break the law, after all." He flashed a sheepish smile that was designed to look innocent, but it left Hannah wondering how he had gotten to Fredericksburg in the first place, if he didn't have a vehicle of his own.

"I appreciate that, but it doesn't change the fact that without some form of identification, I can't rent you a room."

"Oh, well, if that's all..." He dug into his wallet and pulled out an assortment of cards. Most were of the customer loyalty variety. "See here? That's me, Delroy Hatfield."

Hannah reluctantly looked at the cards now scattered over the counter. The man obviously liked his food, as over half of them were to restaurants. One was for a grocery store chain she had never heard of, another was to a miniature golf course. Only the pharmacy discount card looked remotely official. But it was the address on the card—Olathe, Kansas—that made her stand up a bit straighter. *What's taking Walker so long?*

"Again," she said, fingers inching over to locate her phone on the lower desk, "I need some sort of official ID. Something with a photo." She glanced down, making certain her cell was within reach. Could he see over the counter? More importantly, was there a panic button somewhere, like they had in banks? At the moment, it seemed like an excellent idea.

"I gotcha, I gotcha." He went back to dig in his wallet further. After a bit of a struggle, he pried out a worn, plastic-coated employee card and presented it to Hannah with a triumphant smile. "It's an old picture, but that's me, right there in black and white."

She didn't point out that the picture was, in fact, taken in color. Those colors were now faded and weak, but there was no denying the image on the card. He appeared several years younger in the photo and sported not only a full head of hair, but a fuller face. The years had thinned his hair and lined his face, and somewhere along the way, he had dropped at least twenty pounds, but at some point in time, the man named Delroy Hatfield had been employed at *Piedmont Fertilizer Plant*. She held the proof in her hands.

"See? That should do it, won't it?"

A commotion behind her pulled Hannah's attention away from the expectant man.

"We're back!" A singsong voice preceded the flurry into the room. From the sounds of it, both sisters tromped through the hallway from the back door. "And in plenty of time before—oh! You're here!" Surprise rang in Sadie's voice as she rounded the corner and saw the man standing at the front desk. She stopped so abruptly, her sister bumped into her from behind. While Fred grumbled beneath her breath—something about a clumsy ox and a disjointed nose—Sadie beamed at their new guest.

"You made it! Did you have any trouble finding the place? I hope you remembered to eat before you came. Did you try the authentic German place we told you about? I hope you tried the schnitzel. It's to die for." She fired off one sentence after another, never waiting for a response. "Did Hannah get you all checked in? We have your room ready for you. Fred went up earlier and freshened it, just for you. Did you give him the welcome packet, dear?"

Hannah had no idea what a welcome packet was, much less where to find one. She tried to answer, but Sadie didn't stop long enough for her to squeeze a word in.

"You'll have to jiggle your key just a bit, because the lock sticks sometimes. Where's your key? I'll show you what I mean."

Delroy shook his head. "I don't have a key."

"Don't have a key? Why ever not?" Sadie whirled and stared at Hannah in confusion. "Why doesn't this man have a key?"

"Because we're having a bit of a problem checking Mr. Hatfield in." At last having the opportunity to speak, Hannah put as much authority into her voice as she could muster. "It seems he doesn't have a proper form of identification, nor a credit card to secure the room."

"But you just called him Mr. Hatfield, so obviously you know who he is." Spoken with such innocence, the explanation sounded so simple falling from Sadie's lips.

"Yes, but—"

Before Hannah could protest further, Sadie continued. "And Sister and I invited him here."

Hannah scowled, once again torn on how best to handle the Tanner sisters. They had been Miss Wilhelmina's loyal caretakers for years. No doubt the inn's success, however loosely defined, was due in large part to these dedicated women. But Hannah was their boss now, not the other way around. As owner of the property, she should have the ultimate authority on what—and who—was allowed.

She would have said as much had their very first guest not been standing there, watching the silent showdown between the women. And of course, there was the fact Sadie's hazel eyes watered with tears and her face crumpled with vulnerability. She wilted before Hannah's eyes, her bright demeanor fading faster than a sinking sun.

"Of course you did," Hannah said hastily, hoping to put the older woman at ease. "But there's still the matter of payment. Mr. Hatfield doesn't have a credit card."

Fred was the one to speak up. "You have cash, don't you?" she asked the waiting man.

"Sure do!" Instead of digging into his wallet again, Delroy Hatfield reached into the pocket of his t-shirt. He pulled out a handful of wrinkled twenties. "Got cold cash, right here."

"We'll take it!" Fred's matter-of-fact nod gave Hannah no room for protest.

Seething inside, Hannah pushed the clipboard under Hatfield's arm. "You'll need to fill out this paper. Sign at the bottom, and initial everywhere you see an 'x.'" She shot Fred a warning glare, daring her to skip yet another formality. While the man signed as directed, Hannah continued in a stiff voice. "One last signature, in our ledger here, and Fredrika will show you to your room."

"What about breakfast?" the man asked eagerly. "You ladies promised breakfast."

Sadie's smile was once again bright. "Of course we did. Just be down here in the morning, anytime between six and nine, and I'll cook you up a fine meal."

"Out here, or in the kitchen yonder?"

"Here in the dining room," Sadie confirmed.

Fred reached past Hannah and snagged the key, but Hannah failed to notice. She was too busy wondering how Mr. Hatfield knew where the kitchen was. It could be a logical assumption, she supposed, deducing that the kitchen was near the dining room. Yet something about their guest put her on edge. He seemed harmless enough. A bit simple minded, if anything. But she couldn't forget the look in his eyes as he stood outside, surveying the whole of the property. That look was best described as a gleam, and it made her distinctly uncomfortable. It didn't help that he, too, was from Kansas.

Hannah didn't mind admitting, if only to herself, that she was eager for Walker to return.

"Hannah."

Sadie's voice pulled her from her worries. She glanced over at the other woman, surprised to find her looking so contrite.

"Yes?" Fred and Delroy Hatfield were already upstairs, and Hannah hadn't even noticed.

"I realize I overstepped my boundaries just now." Sadie's eyes sunk to the floor, wallowing there with her spirits. "You have to understand, Sister and I have been here our whole lives. We grew up with Wilhelmina. The three of us were thick as thieves, and she always treated us like we were her little sisters. I reckon we sometimes forgot we didn't own the place, just the same as her."

A trace of defiance shone in her eyes as she raised them back to meet Hannah's. Or perhaps it was just emotion. "She encouraged us, she did, letting us run roughshod over the place. It took the three of us to run it, but between us, we made it work. Willie let Sister and I make decisions, same as her, and do pretty much as we pleased." Her chin lifted a fraction of an inch as she continued, "She offered the place to us, you know. Said we deserved it, after dedicating our whole lives to keeping her family's legacy alive. But what would two old spinsters such as us need with a town of our own?" She made a spitting sound, as if casting the very thought from her mouth. "No, it's yours now, fair and square. You can run it as you see fit, and Sister and I need to learn to keep our mouths shut. You'll just have to excuse us, is all. It's hard to break a seventy-year habit, you know."

"Sadie, I want you and Fred to know you'll always have a home here. Even if I hadn't seen the deed, where Miss Wilhelmina gave you the house for as long as either of you were alive, I would never turn you away. I *need* you here. But we're going to have to establish some ground rules." She forced a note of authority into her voice. "You're right, I own this place now, and I have to do what I feel is in the best interest of the inn." Her eyes gravitated to the stairs. "And believe me, that man isn't it. There's something about him that makes me very uncomfortable. We should have turned him away."

"Oh, dear," Sadie said worriedly. "Did I do something terribly wrong?"

"I hope not," Hannah said, her eyes still on the stairs. Fred hadn't come down yet, apparently helping their guest settle in for the night. "But to be honest, I'm just not sure."

CHAPTER 20

When Walker returned, the four of them gathered at the kitchen table for their evening meal.

"The food on the cruise was wonderful," Sadie said dreamily, licking her fingers, "but not even the fanciest dishes compare to Matousek's sausage."

"You sound like that man upstairs," Fred snorted. "To be so close to skinny, all that man talked about was food. Wanted to know if we were serving pork chops for breakfast!" she harrumphed.

Hannah shot Walker a nervous glance. "Pork chops?" Her voice hitched over the words.

"A lot of people have chops for breakfast," Walker reasoned, his voice nice and steady. "Don't make more out of it than it is, Hannah."

"You didn't see the look on his face when he didn't know I was watching. He looked almost... greedy. Just like Everett Tinker." Hannah shivered with the memory.

"Who's Everett Tinker?" Sadie asked.

"That's right, you don't know." Another shiver overtook her. "You tell them, Walker. I'm making coffee."

Walker recapped the events of the past several days, including the missing pork chops and Hank Ruby's unsolved murder. By the time he finished, a solemn silence fell over the table.

"I'm sorry, Hannah. I didn't know." Sadie broke the quietness with her apology. She wrung her hands. "Maybe we should have sent the man away, just like you said."

"Well, it's done now," Fred said in her matter-of-fact manner. "We can't very well turn the man out now. We'll just have to take turns at the desk." Seeing Hannah's confused frown, she explained, "Whenever we have occupants, Sadie and I stay here at the inn. We take turns manning the desk, in case a guest needs something. The other one naps on the couch in the office. We'll do the same tonight, keeping an extra eye out in case our guest decides to wander."

"Well, good luck with that. That couch is now covered in papers after last night's visitor," Hannah reminded them. "And besides, I couldn't ask the two of you to do that."

"You didn't. We volunteered."

Sensing an argument, Walker held up his hand. "I'll settle this. I'll be the one to keep watch. But I do think it's a good idea for you two to stay here tonight."

"You have to work tomorrow. I'll work the desk," Hannah offered.

"We'll all take turns," Sadie decided. "Two-hour shifts, ten to six. Walker can sleep on the couch, in case Mr. Hatfield gets a hankering for pork chops."

With the schedule decided, the sisters cleaned the kitchen while Hannah cleared off the couch. Walker disappeared to take a shower and to prepare for first shift. Too nervous to sleep, Hannah lingered in the office and kept him company for the first hour.

"I don't know if I can do this," she admitted.

"Do what, take third shift? We can switch, if you'd like."

"Seeing as it's almost eleven, that would be cheating. No, I mean I don't know if I can do this whole innkeeper thing. It never occurred to me that I'd be sleeping under the same roof as strangers. I don't know if I can do it."

"You've been doing it for the past two weeks," he pointed out, looking up from his laptop. "You don't know me, not really."

"I know you well enough to know you pose no danger." She flashed a sheepish smile and admitted, "And besides, those first few nights I slept with a candlestick."

He arched a dark brow. "A candlestick?"

"A really heavy candlestick."

"So, go on up to bed and snuggle with your candlestick. Two o'clock comes early, you know."

"I'm serious, Walker. Will it always feel like this?"

He put aside his laptop and focused on her worried face. "You stay at hotels, right? You're essentially doing the same thing then, sleeping under the same roof as strangers."

"But this feels different." She could hear the whine in her own voice but couldn't stop it. "There's more people around at a hotel. Safety of the crowd, and all that."

"I doubt you'll often have a single man staying here, like tonight. More often than not, the inn caters to families." He stood and walked toward her. Settling his hands upon her shoulders, he pushed away a lock of ebony but kept an acceptable distance between them. "After last night's break-in, it's only natural you feel unsettled. Not only that, but you discovered you have ghosts. That's a lot to take on. It would spook anyone, no pun intended."

"I suppose."

"You go on up and try to get some sleep. Between the four of us, we've got this."

"I should feel guilty, expecting two little old ladies to keep me safe."

Walker's eyes danced with merriment. "First of all," he advised, "don't ever let either one of them hear you call them a 'little old lady.' I don't care who they're up against, I'd put my money on either one of them, any day of the week."

A smile played on Hannah's lips. "Got it. And second of all?"

The light shifted in his eyes, darkening into something fluid and warm. Against his better judgment, Walker lifted a long finger to trace the curve of her cheek. "I'll keep you safe, Hannah." He spoke the words as an oath, low and solemn.

Time stuttered between them. Neither moved. Neither dared to breathe, lest they destroy the one perfect moment between them.

Walker broke the spell when he all but growled, "Go to bed, Hannah."

With an overly vigorous nod, she jerked away from the hands resting lightly upon her shoulders. She backed her way out of the office. "Good night, Walker."

The old inn was quiet as she made her way up the stairs. No lights spilled from beneath the bedroom doors. Everyone was in bed. Leroy roamed the perimeter of the property and would no doubt alert them to any danger.

Giving in to the fatigue that came with tension and worry, Hannah crawled into her bed and fell fast asleep.

❧

A noise awoke her. *Probably Fred*, she thought groggily, taking the midnight shift. She turned over and ignored the sound of a door softly shutting.

A few moments later, she heard a thump. She stirred enough to consult her watch. One thirty-eight. Her own shift was coming up in twenty minutes, but that still left twenty more minutes of sleep. Hannah snuggled down deeper into the covers, adjusting the candlestick that shared her pillow.

Another distinct thump. She groaned in protest and tried to ignore the noises out in the hall.

The hall? Coming fully awake, Hannah sat up in bed. Why was someone moving around in the hallway? Fred would never leave her post, and each room had its own private bath, so that ruled out answering the call of nature. If anyone stirred this time of night, it would have to be Delroy Hatfield. Flinging off the covers, Hannah slipped on her shoes, grabbed the candlestick, and eased her door slowly open.

She saw a dark blob inching down the hallway. Every few steps, the blob stopped and tapped on the wall. She assumed the blob was their guest, and she assumed he was looking for a false wall. *What?* she smirked to herself. *Does he think the fabled gold is hidden here at the inn?*

It hit her with staggering force.

Of course! she gasped. That was it! The legend of the hidden treasure.

Judging by his methodical pace down the hall, Hatfield hadn't heard her startled gasp of realization. Hannah shrank back inside her room and allowed the door to shut softly. She tried to recall the specifics of the legend.

An undetermined amount of gold, hidden somewhere nearby. A treasure map, given to the young woman at the stagecoach inn. Hidden, most likely, for safekeeping. Neither, presumably, ever seen again.

How—and why—had the legend suddenly surfaced again, after all these years? Surely that was what Everett Tinker was after, as well, asking about false walls and hidden spaces. It was unlikely that two men happened upon the same old story at the same time, so it stood to reason they were working together. Had it been the two of them in here last night, tearing her new home apart? Had the man in the hallway had a hand in poor Hank Ruby's death, neatly getting the handyman out of the way so that Everett Tinker could come snooping? The very thought made her ill.

Hannah grabbed her phone and sent Walker a text, setting her ringer to silent.

Hatfield roaming hall.

Seconds later, her phone vibrated with a reply. Either the attorney was a very light sleeper, or he was already awake. Reading the text, she had her answer.

Checking out light in dance hall. Stay in room.

Hannah frowned. If Walker was outside, that meant Fred was downstairs by herself. And if Delroy Hatfield was who Hannah suspected he was, he could be a very dangerous man. Despite Walker's earlier declaration, she doubted the seventy-something-year-old Fred was a match for the fortune hunter, some fifteen years her junior.

Hannah knew what she had to do. Sadie was safe, locked within her bedroom, but Hannah's conscious wouldn't allow her to leave Fred downstairs to fend for herself.

She eased her bedroom door open again. Hatfield was at the far end of the hall, his back to her. As quietly as possible, Hannah crept to the staircase and tiptoed onto the top step. It responded with a loud groan. Without stopping to think her actions through, Hannah threw one leg over the banister and pushed herself forward. Holy boomtown, she hoped this hand-rail was as smooth as it looked, or else she would be digging splinters from her back end for days!

The handrail, worn slick from a century worth of caressing hands, offered no protest to her fleece pajama pants. In the time it took for her life to flash before her eyes, Hannah had reached the bottom. It wasn't until she came off the rail that she realized her plan had one major flaw: no landing gear. Airborne for just a moment, the wooden floor soon rushed up to meet her as she crashed upon it in an undignified heap.

"Hannah!" Fred gasped in surprise. "What on earth—!"

"Shh!" Lying flat on her back, not entirely certain that no bones were broken, Hannah hissed out the warning. She motioned upward, expecting to see Delroy Hatfield appear at any moment. Fred hurried over to help her up, half-dragging her along the floor. It was the quickest way to get her out of sight.

"What's going on?" Fred whispered.

"Hatfield is in the hallway, snooping around."

"No, somehow he slipped out of his room and made it over to the old saloon. Walker is out there now."

"That's his partner. Come to think of it, I should warn Walker." She shot off a quick message while still sitting in the floor. She wasn't sure her legs would hold her.

"Hatfield has a partner? How do you know that? And what's he doing in the hallway?"

"Help me to the kitchen, and I'll tell you about it. I think I may need to put some ice on this ankle." When Fred would have fussed over her ankle, now swollen and throbbing, Hannah motioned her away. "Just help me to the kitchen."

Hopping was too noisy, hobbling too painful. In the end, Hannah scooted her way across the hall. Fred alternated between pushing and pulling, until they were both safely ensconced inside the kitchen.

"*Now* will you tell me what's going on?" Fred huffed. She filled a zip-lock bag with ice, wrapped it inside a faded kitchen towel, and placed it on Hannah's ankle, which was now propped upon the table.

Hannah winced when the cold sensation touched her skin. "I think I know what they're after. I think they're searching for the hidden treasure."

"Hidden treasure! You mean the old legend?"

"Yes. For whatever reason, the two men going by the names of Delroy Hatfield and Everett Tinker think the old legend is true, and they've come here to search for it. That's the only explanation. You should have seen Tinker, tapping on every surface and asking about false floors and fake walls. And upstairs right now, Hatfield is tapping himself silly, hoping to find a hidden panel of some kind. And you saw what they did to the office."

"But that legend is more than a hundred years old!"

"Why else would those two men be here, trying to tear the place apart? Seriously, Tinker wanted to tear the inn down."

"He wouldn't dare!" Fred huffed. With her hands upon her hips and her green eyes flashing, she looked like five feet two inches of dynamite, ready to explode.

"We should call 9-1-1. Where's my phone?" Hannah looked all around, but her cell was nowhere in sight. "I must have left it out there on the floor. Hand me the portable, will you?"

Fred picked up the cordless phone and pressed the 'on' button. When nothing happened, she gave it a shake. "Either the battery's dead or the phone lines are down."

"You'll have to get my phone. I wonder what's keeping Walker so long. I wish he'd hurry."

"Leroy was barking up a storm, so Walker looked out to see what the fuss was about. He thought he saw a light moving through the saloon. He went to investigate."

Worry snagged at Hannah's heart. "I hope he's careful," she said.

"He took his gun. You stay here, and I'll be back in a flash."

While Fred slipped silently from the room, Hannah closed her eyes for a moment of respite. She hurt in a dozen places, her ankle being the worst. Good thing she didn't think it was broken; terms of the stipulation wouldn't allow her to go for x-rays.

She heard rustling in the doorway. Reluctant to open her eyes, she whispered, "Fred, is that you?"

The voice that answered was much too low to belong to Fred. So low, in fact, that it could only belong to a man. "No," someone whispered back.

Hannah jerked her eyes open and stared into the leering grin of Everett Tinker. His large, overall-clad body filled the doorway. His booming voice filled the room. "Well, looks like you've done gone and got yourself hurt, don't you know."

"What are you doing here?" Hannah demanded. She would have lowered her leg, but it was like moving a log. Her limb, practically numbed from poor circulation, felt heavy and stiff.

"I came to claim what rightfully belongs to my great-granddaddy, Maurice Hatfield."

Hannah stared at the man in surprise. "Patch Hatfield was your grandfather?" she squeaked.

"Great-grandfather, don't you know. All our lives, Big Daddy told us about him, and what a good man he was. Told us how that gold belonged to him, fair and square, until that medicine woman put a curse on him. Ran him out of the country, she did, and wouldn't let him come back to claim the spoils of victory. But the curse died with the old woman, don't you know. So now we're here to claim it, and this time, we ain't leaving until we find it."

"That's just some silly legend," Hannah insisted. She couldn't resist crinkling her nose and adding, "Don't you know."

"It ain't legend, it's fact! And I got the letter to prove it!" He pulled a dog-eared envelope from his pocket. The paper was spotted with age and frayed around the edges, with tiny holes and deep creases to mark the passage of time. "Here. Read it for yourself!" he challenged.

Hannah cringed when he came close enough to hand the letter to her, but he moved back to allow her room. Nerves made her hands unsteady as she pulled the crumbling letter from its holder.

"It's so faded, I can hardly read it," she murmured. She barely made out the greeting, written in flowing, curly script. She could detect the words 'my dearest Maurice,' but the first few sentences were almost illegible. After a moment of concentration, she caught the gist of the letter. Lina had the map and would keep it safe, until her beloved came back to claim it. And her. She made out the words 'chest' and 'treasure,' but they weren't in the same sentence, and the words between them were blurred. The most legible part of the letter was the ending, with its profession of undying love and the signature 'My heart is forever yours, Lina Hannah.'

"See?" Everett all but crowed. "That's proof, right there. Proof there was a treasure, and it's hidden somewhere on this property! I'll tear the whole dang place apart if I have to, until I find that treasure chest!"

A noisy commotion erupted in the hallway and made its way into the kitchen. Delroy Hatfield pushed Fred into the room and gave her a shove that almost sent her toppling.

"Well, well, looks like we're having ourselves a party!" Everett said with a leering grin.

To Hannah's surprise, Fred straightened her small frame, narrowed her eyes, and fairly spat at the big man. "Bigs Hatfield, what are you doing back here!"

He merely grinned at her outburst. "I remember you. You're still a fine-lookin' woman, even after all these years. I came back to claim my treasure, don't you know."

"Wilhelmina threw you out years ago and warned you to never come back!"

Both Hannah and Delroy were confused by the turn of conversation. Delroy was the first to speak up. "What's she talking about, Bigs? You been here before? But the curse..."

"Once, don't you know, back in the late sixties. I was on a job down in San Antone, so I made a little detour. This whole place was run by women, don't you know, including the Hannah woman, that one whose family put the curse on ours. I didn't do nothing, just tried to reason with them."

Fred snorted. "More like you tried to threaten us, but Wilhelmina set you straight. Sent you packing, all the way back to Kansas."

Bigs' face colored with anger. He didn't like being reminded of his failure, particularly in front of his brother. "But I'm back now, and this time, I ain't backing down. I ain't leaving, till I find the gold that little gal hid!"

"You old fool, she hid the map, not the treasure."

"Fine! Then I'll tear this place apart until I find the map. And you ladies are going to help me!"

"Says who?" Fred sassed, hands upon her hips.

"Says me and my Colt." Bigs Hatfield reached into his baggy overalls and produced a gun. He pointed it at the older woman, motioning for her to move. "Get over by your friend so I can keep an eye on you."

"You know Walker is right outside," Hannah reminded the men. "He'll be back at any moment."

"I ain't worried 'bout him," Bigs, aka Everett Tinker, said with an evil grin. "Me and my Colt done had our conversation with him."

"You killt him?" Delroy squeaked, his eyes popping wide. "You said no more killing!"

"Shut up, Delroy! I didn't kill him, least ways I don't think I did. Knocked him over the head is all. Now shut up and find us something to eat."

At the mention of food, his brother brightened. He eagerly made his way to the refrigerator, no longer concerned about the possibility of another death on their count. "They do have some fine eating here. Maybe they have some more pork chops." He rubbed his hands together in anticipation.

Hannah had been in the process of easing her leaden leg back down to the floor. She paused in the process to exclaim, "Pork chops! It was you, wasn't it?"

"I swear, those were the best pork chops I ever did eat. Say, maybe you could give me the r—"

Before he could finish his sentence, Bigs whipped off his cap and swatted his brother. While he berated the foolish notion of swapping recipes while under gunpoint, not to mention in the middle of searching for lost treasure, Fred slipped Hannah her cell phone. She then made a show of helping Hannah adjust the ice pack to her ankle, providing effective cover while Hannah shot off a text to 9-1-1. Not that the arguing brothers even noticed, particularly when Delroy opened the refrigerator and found the leftover sausage.

"Maybe I'll skip California," Del said, talking with his mouth full, "and settle down here. These Texans sure know how to eat."

Bigs stuffed a fat link into his mouth, wiping the grease from his mouth with the back of his hand. "That they do, little brother. But when we're done here, we won't be sticking around."

"Why not?" Del whined. "I like it here. And I sure would like to meet up with that pretty little blond gal again. She sure can cook." He looked around the kitchen, as if expecting to see her.

"His light is even dimmer than his brother's," Fred muttered from the side of her mouth. "What blonde is he talking about?"

"Caroline." Hannah saw Fred's eyebrows shoot upward. "Yes," she whispered, "I know about Caroline. And no, Delroy doesn't." Despite the serious situation they were in, a giggle escaped her lips.

"Hey!" Bigs barked, jerking his attention back to the two women he more or less held a gun upon. In actuality, the barrel pointed down and off to the side as he devoured another sausage. "What's so funny over there?"

"Just the two of you, Bigs," Fred said, seemingly unconcerned with the danger of goading him. "Thinking there's still a fortune to be found. If we knew where the map was, don't you think we would have already claimed the fortune for ourselves?"

Both men narrowed their eyes, considering the possibility of her words. Again, it was almost amusing, watching the time it took for their thoughts to compute. When they finally did, Delroy's face crinkled with concern, while Bigs' face contorted in rage.

"You stole our fortune?" Bigs bellowed. "All our life, we've waited for the old lady to die, waited to get our hands on the fortune, and now we're here, and you tell us it's already gone?"

"I said no such thing!" snapped Fred.

Hannah could see the situation was getting out of hand. Bigs was angry, Fred's saucy attitude only made matters worse, and Delroy, once again digging in the refrigerator, threatened to eat them into starvation.

"Out of curiosity," Hannah quickly interjected, hoping to cut the tension in the room, "what does Miss Wilhelmina's death have to do with this? Why were you waiting for her to die?"

"Because she was the last of the Hannah family. When she died, so did the curse on our family."

"What curse was that?"

"That medicine woman put some sort of hex on our great-granddaddy for breaking that Hannah gal's heart, don't you know. Cursed us for all generations. But with the Hannah bloodline now gone, there's no more need for the hex. It frees our family from the curse, once and for all, don't you know." His eyes lit with greed and a smile spread across his fleshy face. "And with the curse out of the way"—he spread his arms wide in a gesture of freedom—"we're free to come back here and search for the gold."

"Except for extending the curse."

Bigs did a double take at her words. "Huh?" A dumbfounded expression filled his face.

Hannah nodded her head vigorously, hoping to sound convincing when she said, "You ignored the curse and came back anyway, back in... when was it?" She looked to Fred for confirmation.

"Sixty-nine."

"Okay, that was almost fifty years ago, so naturally, that extends the curse by another fifty years."

"Is that true?" Delroy poked his head out from behind the refrigerator door, losing interest in the cold noodles. "Bigs, did you do that?" His voice hitched higher. "Did you extend the curse?"

"No! No, of course not! She's making that up!" his brother claimed, but he didn't look—nor sound—so sure of the fact.

"Come on, Bigs," Fred put in, "everyone knows this. If you ignore a curse, you simply prolong it."

"She's lying!" Bigs jabbed his beefy finger toward Hannah, his eyes going wild. "You're lying!"

"No, I'm not. And I can prove it, too."

CHAPTER 21

Hannah grabbed her cell phone and tapped several keys.

"Whoa, whoa, whoa. What'd ya think you're doing?" Bigs demanded.

"Why, I'm pulling it up on my cell phone." Hannah batted her eyelashes for added credibility. "You can find anything on the web. Don't you know."

His eyes narrowed. "You ain't trying to trick us, are you?"

Pressing the 'send' button, Hannah looked Bigs straight in the eye. And lied. "Of course not."

She hurriedly pulled up the internet and pressed a few keys. "Here it is right here. No, never mind, that's not it... Okay, it says here... no, that's not it, either. Just give me a second. I know I saw this, just the other day..."

"Let me tell you something, little girl," Bigs snarled. "If you're messing with us, this Colt here will put a curse on you that ain't *never* gonna come off."

Hannah gave him her best wide-eyed stare. "You're holding a gun on us. Why would I mess with you?"

Standing a bit taller, Bigs puffed out his chest as he fell for her flattery. "You best remember that, too," he sniffed.

"Absolutely." She batted her blue eyes and covertly pressed another button, sending Walker a brief text.

You OK? In kitchen. Gun.

"Well? We ain't got all day! What's that fancy little phone of yours say about the rules of a curse?" Bigs demanded.

"I'm still looking for it..."

"Come to think of it," Fred suddenly pitched in, "didn't you tell me you found that in one of the books in the office?" With her head turned just so, the men couldn't see the coded look in her eyes.

"Aah... Yes, maybe that was it," Hannah decided. "Maybe it was in one of those big books." *Those big, heavy books. The kind heavy enough to do some damage upside a man's head.* "But my ankle..."

"Del, take Freddie in the office and look for a book on curses," Bigs directed, unwittingly playing into their hand. He motioned to Hannah with his gun. "You keep looking on your phone."

"I'm sure one of us will find it," she claimed with false optimism. She sent one more brief text, before pulling up a search on how to cast a curse. To her surprise, the page populated with thousands of hits. "Oh, my," she murmured.

"What? What does it say?"

She heard the worry in Bigs' voice and played upon it. "This isn't good," she murmured, pretending to read from the screen. "Not good at all. Let me try another site."

The big man paced the floor. He muttered to himself, but Hannah caught occasional snippets of his rant. Apparently, Big Daddy, whomever that was, had warned them. Curses weren't to be taken lightly. He rattled on about bad luck and lost jobs and not getting that pony when he was ten, all because of some old Indian woman. When he began to moan about Hank Ruby and the lawyer and being forced into it, Hannah grew concerned.

Walker hadn't replied yet, meaning he must be seriously injured. Her mind wouldn't consider the possibility of it being anything worse. Knowing she had to check on him, she came up with a new plan. By the time she executed it, the police should have arrived.

"I just realized something." Her sudden announcement stopped Bigs in his tracks.

"What? You found an anecdote? Something to stop the curse, even if I extended it?"

"No, this isn't about the curse. This is better," she bluffed. "I think I may know where the map is hidden."

"Where? Tell me!"

"I'll take you there."

He looked suspiciously at her leg. "What about your ankle?"

"It's better now, see?" She hopped to her feet, biting back the howl of pain before it could make a liar of her. Turning a grimace into a forced smile, she said through clenched teeth, "A—All better."

"Where are we going?"

"F—Follow me." She steeled herself to the pain and led the way out of the kitchen.

"Tell me where we're going, or I'll shoot you now!"

Hannah stopped to lean against a chair in the big room. Not because she believed his threats, but because she needed the breather. Despite her pain, her voice came out cool and even. "Then you'll never know, will you?"

He grumbled and motioned for her to continue, balking only when he realized where they headed. "You're headed to the saloon, ain't cha? You're trying to trick me. You just want to check on your boyfriend."

In too much pain to elaborate, Hannah managed a terse, "Yes, saloon. No, boyfriend."

"Hold on here now," Bigs sputtered, but Hannah ignored him and kept going. If she stopped now, she might fall. Best to keep moving while she could.

Reaching the saloon, Hannah fell against the rails of the porch and caught her breath. From the looks of the large man huffing and puffing behind her, he needed to do the same thing. After a brief breather, she summoned the strength to stand again on her throbbing ankle and pushed the door open. She flipped the lights on and immediately searched for Walker, fearing the worst.

It was bad, but not in the way she expected.

"Where'd he go?" Bigs bellowed, barging through the door behind her. He pointed to an empty spot on the floor, smeared with something that could only be blood. "He was right there, crumpled over like a sack of potatoes!"

Panting in pain and exhaustion, Hannah caught her breath as she wailed to herself. *Great! I hobble all this way out here to make sure he's still breathing, and he's not even here. He's probably sneaking back to the kitchen, thinking he'll rescue me. Now what do I do?*

"Never mind the lawyer," Bigs said, grabbing her arm and twisting. "Tell me where the map is!"

"Right there on the wall."

He glanced behind him, at the row of framed photographs and posters. "Ain't no map up there," he snorted. "You messing with me, girl? Because I done warned you—"

It was Hannah's turn to snort. "Of course it's not right there in plain sight, for just anyone to see. Don't any of those faces look familiar to you?"

He stood back and scanned the wall. "I see Elvis and Willie Nelson. Lyle Lovett. Don't know some of those other bands."

"What about the Wanted posters?"

While Bigs stepped closer to examine the smaller posters, Hannah looked around for a weapon of some sort. There was nothing within reach, not even a chair she could crash over his head. What if she broke the glass in one of the pictures and held it to his neck? She immediately discarded the idea, knowing he was stronger than she. There had to be something...

"Why, that there is my great-granddaddy, Patch Hatfield!" Bigs crowed in pleasure. "And look at how much he was worth, dead or alive! He really was famous. A true American legend."

Hannah didn't point out that he may have been a legend, but not in a heroic way. The man was an outlaw. His 'worth,' as Bigs called it, was measured only by the price his would-be captors were willing to pay to put him behind bars or in the ground.

Bigs took the framed poster down and held it as tenderly as if it were a newborn child. Were those tears in the big man's eyes?

"Just like Big Daddy always said," he cooed.

Hannah inched toward the door, her first few steps undetected. When a board squeaked beneath her feet, Bigs jerked his head up from his reverie.

"Where do you think you're going, missy?"

"I was going to give you a minute," Hannah offered. "I know this is a proud moment for you. I'll just wait outside."

He brushed his knuckles beneath one eye and shook his head. "It is, but never mind about that. Just tell me where the map is."

Time was running out, and she still hadn't heard the wail of sirens. And where, by the way, was Leroy when she needed him?

Bigs' face hardened with impatience. "I asked you where the map was!"

"Well, obviously, you're holding it."

"Huh?"

As she started to explain, she heard Leroy bark. By the time she finished her hastily contrived explanation, the dog was making quite a ruckus. It sounded like it was coming from the empty cabin next door.

"Well, it stands to reason that Lina Hannah would hide the map behind the picture of the man she loved, the man who had, in fact, helped to steal the treasure in the first place. Your great-grandfather, Patch Hatfield."

"Right here?" Bigs asked in wonder, turning the frame over in his hands. "But I don't see it."

"She would have put it inside, don't you think? Under glass and behind the wanted poster. But you'll have to be careful, and go slow," Hannah cautioned. "They're very old papers, you know. They'll tear easily. You'd better use the table."

"That crazy dog won't shut up!" Bigs complained as he carried the frame to the nearest table. "I shoulda shot him when I had the chance, instead of just shutting him up in that cabin."

Bigs bent over the back of the frame, his hands trembling with excitement.

Hannah took a small step backwards.

He eased the metal prongs up, the ones that held the backboard in place.

Hannah retreated another step.

"I can't believe I'm this close," he whispered, carefully setting aside the backboard.

Even with her hurt and throbbing ankle, Hannah increased her stride and moved one giant pace closer to the door.

"Lina Hannah thought she was so smart, keeping the treasure hidden from my family all these years, but I'll show her, don't you know."

His hand touched paper. Any moment, he would turn it over and realize it was only the wanted poster. He would whirl around and find her there, just steps away from freedom.

Hannah had to hurry. She slid another step backward, preparing to take another.

A man's voice stopped her, but it wasn't Bigs speaking.

"You fool," the voice said bitterly. "Lina didn't keep the treasure from your family. She *saved* it for you, hoping Patch would come back for it. For her. She pined her life away for that fool of a man. And she carried the secret of the hidden treasure to her grave."

"Huh? Who said that?" Bigs jerked his head up. He whirled to his left, searching for the man behind the voice. He turned right, still looking for the speaker. He finally turned around, and spotted Hannah there, almost to the door.

"So *close!*" she moaned beneath her breath.

"Who said that?" Bigs demanded.

She tried looking innocent. Maybe she could get him refocused, and still make her escape. "Who said what? Did you find the map? You didn't tear it, did you?"

"You didn't hear that man talking? He called my great-granddaddy a fool!"

"It was probably just the dog whining, or the wind. You know these old buildings." Hannah motioned toward the frame. "Be careful when you lift the map out. The paper is very old, you know."

It almost worked.

Bigs nodded and turned back around, eager to finish his discovery. Hannah released her held breath and slid backwards. One more step, and she was out the door.

"Your great-grandfather was a coward and a fool, and he didn't deserve a fine woman like my Lina," the voice said again. Fully dismayed, Hannah looked back and saw the ghost of Orlan Varela moving out from the shadows, the vision still weak and wispy. His voice, however, was strong. "He ran away the first chance he got, and he never came back for her. He broke his promise to her, and he broke her heart."

"There was a hex." Bigs defended the slant against his grandfather, even though he couldn't see the man making the accusations. He looked around in confusion. "Where are you? Where's that voice coming from?" His eyes zeroed in on Hannah, and how her hand was posed to open the door. "Get back over here!" he bellowed. He turned to get the gun, but it was no longer there on the table. "Huh? Where'd it go?" He bent to see if it had fallen.

"Over here," Orlan taunted him. "Another foolish Hatfield, I see."

Bigs whirled around, until he had turned his large body in a complete circle. He reminded Hannah of a dog, chasing its tail. "Who's there?" he demanded. Bigs swung his large fists, swatting at air. "Come out here where I can see you! Make your insults like a man, not like a coward."

"You mean like your great-grandfather."

"You know diddly about my great-granddaddy! He had to go back. There was a hex on him, don't you know." Bigs took on a boxer's stance, the treasure map all but forgotten. "Now come out here, so's I can fight you."

"I'm right here," Orlan said, materializing before Bigs' eyes.

"Huh? Wh—Where'd you come from?"

Orlan ignored the question and addressed his earlier claim. "You are wrong. I know a great deal about your great-grandfather. I know *him*, in fact. Or, I did." The ghost lifted his head with pride. "And *I* am the one responsible for the curse upon your family. I asked the Great Spirits for help so I could keep my beloved Lina safe, even from death."

Bigs Hatfield blanched two shades beyond pale. His eyes bulged within their sockets and his mouth fell open. He mumbled some unintelligible babble. He finally managed a painful gulp of air. "B—B—But you're a—a—"

"A ghost. Is this the word you search for?"

Bigs could barely manage a nod.

"Orlan Varela." The vaquero ghost introduced himself with a distinguished bow. "Just before my death, I had the honor of making Lina Hannah my bride, but it was in name only. Alas, her heart belonged to the scoundrel you call your great-granddaddy. He never deserved her love, or her undying loyalty." If possible, the ghost gave the other man a scathing look. His voice took on a cold air that frosted the entire room. "You dishonor her good name. And for that, you, sir, shall be cursed until death."

"No! No, anything but that!" Bigs begged. He put both arms up to his head in a protective stance. "No! Don't go! Don't leave me here, cursed till death!"

As the ghost's image faded away, the big man fell to his knees. His pleas faded into sobs. "Don't go. Don't do this to me!" he begged in a pitiful whimper.

The gun appeared on the floor near Hannah's feet. She stooped to retrieve it, knowing she had Orlan to thank. It felt heavy and clumsy in her hand, but she picked it up and pointed it at the pathetic man groveling nearby.

"Get up, Bigs," she said, her voice not unkind. Thief or not—most likely even a murderer, when the truth was revealed—the man was having a meltdown before her very eyes. No one should ever witness such a thing.

"Hannah! Hannah, are you okay?" Walker burst through the door, his gun drawn and already centered upon Bigs Hatfield. "Did he hurt you?"

Her smile wavered as she glanced down at her throbbing ankle. "No, but I managed to hurt myself. Anyway, you're the one who's bleeding. Are you okay?"

He put a hand to his forehead and swiped at the trickle of blood making its way down his brow. He only managed to smear it worse than it already was. "I'm fine," he insisted. "Other than a headache."

"We need to get back to the inn. His brother has Fred."

Despite his injury, Walker pulled off an incredibly sexy grin. "Actually, it's the other way around. Fred and Sadie have things well in hand, just like I told you they would." He walked over to Bigs, pulled on his arm, and hauled the sobbing man to his feet. "Get up, Tinker, or whatever your name is."

"Hatfield," Hannah supplied. "Bigs Hatfield, great-grandson of the notorious Patch Hatfield."

"Figures," Walker said with a grunt of disapproval. He shoved the man forward but didn't release his arm. "March." His tone was unyielding. With a more conciliatory glance down at Hannah, he asked, "Can you walk?"

"I'll manage."

She hobbled out to the porch and waited there, while Walker marched Bigs to the cabin next door and freed Leroy.

With Leroy's help—the dog held a grudge, barking and nipping at Bigs' heels the whole way—Walker guided the man back to the inn. Hannah lagged behind, half-hopping, half-shuffling her way across the drive. She reached the front door, about the same time two sheriffs' vehicles came screeching up the gravel path, their sirens deafening in the still night air.

"Sadie!" Hannah called as she crossed the threshold. "Fred! Are you okay?"

"In here!"

Hannah hobbled her way through the front room. Sadie's gray head poked from the kitchen door. "Come on back," she called, "I'm making kolaches for breakfast. And the coffee's already on."

"Coffee? I need whiskey!"

Fred came from the office, a decanter already in her hand. "One step ahead of you," she said, crossing through the hall to the kitchen. She stopped and turned back. "Do you need help?"

"I've come this far, I can make it the rest of the way," Hannah claimed. As Fred went on about her way, Hannah added beneath her breath, "I hope."

A few more hopped steps, and she made it to the kitchen door. She collapsed into the nearest chair, even before taking stock of the sight before her.

Sadie kneaded out a ball of dough, punching and poking to get the texture just right. Fred carefully poured a measure of whiskey into a steaming cup of coffee. And behind them, tied to a straight-back chair by an array of colorful aprons and kitchen twine, was a groggy, half-conscious Delroy Hatfield.

Unable to help herself, Hannah burst out in laughter.

Fred turned to her with a look of utter innocence. "What?" she asked.

"You—You two!" Hannah cackled. "You *three*!" she corrected. "What—What did you do to him?"

"Exactly what you said, dear," Sadie said. "I got your text, so I came downstairs, found my heaviest rolling pin, and while Fred distracted him, I conked him over the head. Then we dragged him in here and tied him up."

"I—I said to stall him, until 9-1-1 got here." Hannah laughed so hard tears leaked from her eyes.

Sadie shrugged one shoulder and tossed the man a sorry look. "Same difference." She dusted off her hands and clamored around the kitchen until she found the baking pan she was looking for. "Hope you're hungry. After the night we had, we all deserve a feast!"

CHAPTER 22

It was a feast, indeed. Kolaches filled with peach preserves or sweetened cream cheese. Thick slices of bacon, alongside platters of fried eggs, biscuits, and a bowl of gravy. Fresh fruit and grits. Plenty of coffee—with or without the whiskey—and fresh milk.

"I can't move," Hannah moaned. "I'm not even sure I can breathe."

"Is your foot still up?" Sadie asked, hovering over her like a mother hen. "The doctor said to keep it up for the rest of the day. And Walker, he said for you to rest. You should go upstairs and lie down."

"Not after that meal, I shouldn't," the attorney protested. Even with the white bandage around his head, he looked disturbingly handsome. Much too handsome for Hannah's comfort, at any rate.

Breakfast had to wait until after the doctor made his house call. He diagnosed Hannah's ankle as sprained and Walker's head as hard. With a day or two of rest, he predicted both would be as good as ever.

"Well," said Fred, clapping her hands together, "now that we have two men arrested, a murder solved, two patients healing, breakfast over and done, and our fair share of excitement for the month, what do we have planned for the day?"

"Rest!" the other three answered in unison.

"Rest? But my adrenaline is still pumping!" the older woman proclaimed. "I don't think I could just sit back and *rest* for the remainder of the day."

"Fine," her sister snorted. "I did most of the cooking. You can do the dishes."

"I'll keep you company," Hannah offered. In truth, she was too full to move, and she had finally found a comfortable position for her foot.

The sisters cleared the table, and soon, Walker's phone rang. As word of the morning's events spread, his cell phone sang out with a steady jingle. He set the ringer to silent during their meal, but some of the calls couldn't be ignored. When a client called for the third time, Walker left the table with a grumble and said he would be in his room, after all. He would take the rest of his calls upstairs.

Sadie made a point of listening for Walker's door to close. "Ah, finally," she said, looking pleased.

"Walker is a fine man—" Fred started.

"—and easy on the eye," Sadie interrupted.

"—but it's time for a little girl talk."

Hannah knew the sisters had something important on their mind. They converged upon the table like ants at a picnic. Before Hannah had time to feel nervous, Fred slid a tattered envelope her way. "We thought you might like this."

She recognized it immediately. "This is the letter Lina Hannah wrote!"

"I found it here on the table," Sadie explained. "Bigs must have left it."

Hannah's eyes lit with excitement. "We should frame this! We could hang it here in the inn, so that guests see it when they check in."

Neither sister shared her enthusiasm. Their puckered brows confused her.

"I'm not sure you want to do that, dear." Sadie's voice was slightly reproachful.

"Why not? It's an important piece of history."

Fred seemed to choose her words carefully. "Folks around here have heard the legend of hidden treasure for over a hundred years."

Sadie nodded in agreement. "But that's all it was. A legend."

"But this letter changes things," her sister continued. "With this letter, the legend becomes truth. Rumors become facts."

"There were enough fortune hunters before, when it was nothing but a fabled tale. But if the truth ever got out..."

"We would be overrun with tourists!" Fred's voice was aghast.

"Forgive me for sounding obtuse," Hannah broke in gently, "but wouldn't that be a good thing? This is a hotel, after all. We want tourists." When both sisters looked slightly horrified, Hannah's voice took on a questionable note. "Don't we?"

"Tourists are one thing, dear," Sadie pointed out. "Treasure hunters are quite another."

"Just look at the Hatfield brothers," her sister added smartly. "No need in encouraging the likes of men like Bigs and Delroy Hatfield. Why, folks would flock here in droves, poking around and digging holes, and sticking their noses into places they don't belong."

Sadie's gray head bobbled up and down. "No need in stirring up a hornet's nest and shooing the buzz our way."

"I see your point," Hannah murmured, "but I'm not sure Walker will. He manages the money, you know."

"About that..."

"As we said, Walker is a wonderful man, but he's..."

"A lawyer," Fred finished bluntly. "A fine one at that, and honest to a fault. Too honest to keep the letter to himself, if he knew about it."

Hannah stared down at the century-old envelope. "That's right, he didn't see this." Another thought occurred to her. "But... isn't this evidence? Shouldn't we turn this over to the sheriff?"

Fred lifted a delicate shoulder. She was once again dressed in a smart, western-styled outfit, complete with the mammoth belt buckle. Having traded yesterday's Hawaiian shirt for a simple housedress, Sadie attempted a nonchalant shrug of her own.

"Walker would probably see it that way," she allowed. "But you know as well as we do, if anyone knew you had that letter, you'd likely never see it again. They might use it in court."

"Even worse, they might confiscate it and add it to the county museum. Lord knows we'd never keep it secret then!"

Hannah eyed the sisters with suspicion. "Keep what secret? What aren't you telling me?"

"Why, that the legend is real, of course," Fred said, but she turned so that Hannah couldn't quite see her face.

Eyes narrowed, Hannah pulled the letter from its envelope and carefully smoothed out the folds. Without touching the paper more than necessary—she knew oils from her skin could further damage the old document—she reread the faded words. Her attention snagged in the next-to-last paragraph, when Lina wrote about a chest. Once again, Hannah thought it odd that it was in a separate sentence than the mention of treasure; the two normally went hand in hand, as in *treasure chest.*

She read the letter again, and then a third time. When she raised her eyes, both sisters tried hard to look casual. Fred gave special attention to the non-existent wrinkles she smoothed from her shirt, while Sadie scrubbed her nail against a long since set-in stain upon the tablecloth.

"Lina was quite talented, wasn't she?" Hannah remarked quietly.

"Oh, she was a fine letter writer!" Sadie readily agreed. "Very talented when it came to words."

"She was talented with a paintbrush, too. I saw her paintings. In a time when most young women were stitching samplers and perfecting their sewing skills, it struck me as odd that Lina preferred to spend her time painting. She was quite the artist."

"Those were done when she was quite a bit older," Fred clarified. "She spent her days painting and daydreaming, pining her life away for that no-good Hatfield. Other than her token deathbed marriage to poor Orlan Varela, Lina never married. She died an old maid."

"I saw the green chest in my room. The room that once belonged to Miss Wilhelmina." Hannah kept her voice slow and even, watching the sisters' faces as she spoke. "I believe Lina painted that when she was rather young. Shortly after Patch Hatfield disappeared, in fact."

Sadie cleared her throat.

Fred averted her eyes and murmured a casual, "Oh?"

"You two can stop trying to look so innocent," Hannah informed them. "I know what happened."

"What do you mean, dear?"

Hannah leaned in and admonished the older ladies. "Come on, we're having a girl talk. You can at least be honest with me. I know that Lina Hannah painted the map onto the green chest, essentially hiding it in plain sight. And even though the markings don't mean anything to me —a crooked tree, a bird, a field of flowers, a triangle— they meant something to Wilhelmina, didn't they?"

Sadie's eyes flew to meet her sister's. Together, they turned their surprised gazes upon the younger woman. "What are you saying?"

"This letter is badly faded, but it appears Lina is telling Patch about a chest she painted, and the pretty *markings* she put on it. She doesn't directly say she painted the map onto the chest, but it makes sense that she did."

"That would have been rather smart of her." Fred's murmur was noncommittal.

Sadie patted Hannah's hand and added, "And smart of you, to figure it out like that."

Hannah wasn't finished. "That's not all I figured out," she announced quietly. She took their silence as an invitation to continue. "When Bigs said he came here in the late sixties, I remembered the entry I saw in the ledgers. In 1970, Miss Wilhelmina made a sizable deposit at the bank. About a year later, she made another large deposit."

Still no response from the sisters.

"She found the treasure, didn't she?" Hannah pressed.

Sadie gave a breezy, "We wouldn't know, dear."

Hannah scrutinized them both, her eyes narrowed. "Actually, I think you would, because I think the two of you helped her."

Fred put her hand to her chest in a gesture of innocence. "What are you saying? You think Bigs Hatfield came here and foolishly showed us that letter, confirming what we had always suspected about that green chest and its artwork? How do you think we would have been able to find those landmarks after almost a century had passed? Why, we would have had to spend an entire winter down at the historical society, going through old journals and letters. Grainy old photographs, too."

"That's right." Sadie bobbed in agreement. "We would have had to talk to old timers and neighbors, just to understand some of those landmarks. How would we have known the triangle was a teepee, or where the old Indian campground was? How would we have deciphered the black birds? We wouldn't have known that Homer Myer's grandfather used to keep a field of corn, about a half mile from the double curve in Grape Creek. We had no way of knowing it was notorious for attracting crows, and that Lina would paint them as one of the clues. That field was long gone by the fall of '70!"

Even though Hannah had figured most of it out for herself, the reality still amazed her. She stared at her new friends in fascination. "So, you're telling me that the three of you realized the map was painted on the chest, spent almost a year deciphering the landmarks, and went out and found the hidden treasure, all by yourselves?"

Sadie took a sudden interest in the ceiling, while Fred studied her shirt pocket.

When Fred finally spoke, her denial sounded quite sincere. "We aren't telling you a thing, dear. This is your story."

"Why on earth would we tell you something that could possibly land us all in hot water?" Sadie asked, her wide eyes equally innocent. "I don't know, mind you, but suppose there isn't a statute of limitation on the recovery of the gold? Suppose it technically still belongs to the Army. Why, if we made some ridiculous claim about finding that gold and not returning it, it would be almost as if we stole it ourselves."

"And if you, Hannah, knew about it and didn't turn us in, it could make you an accessory," reasoned her sister. "So why would we tell you we were involved in something like that, when it could get us all in trouble?"

"That's right, dear. And as far as we know, that's just an old green chest in your room."

Fred gave a shrug of her shoulders. "And with no proof to back it up—"

"—certainly without a letter, written in Lina's own hand—"

"—the artwork is just the fanciful musings of a young artist."

Hannah stared hard at the sisters. One thing still troubled her. "Walker doesn't know?"

Fred was the one to answer, but she chose her words carefully. "Let's say Wilhelmina did choose to share personal secrets with him. Not only is it none of our business, but it probably falls under some client confidentiality clause. Why stir up a hornet's nest? I say 'don't ask, don't tell.'"

Hannah refolded the letter and carefully returned it to the envelope. "So, you're suggesting we keep this between us?"

"Considering everything we've just told you, I think it's best, don't you?"

Sadie turned watery hazel eyes to Hannah and spoke from her heart. "If Walker ever reads that letter, he'll come to the same conclusions you did. I have no idea about statutes of limitation, but that boy upstairs is good as gold, and he was a godsend to three old women when we needed him the most. We'll not risk putting him in the thick of all this and force him to compromise his values, not to save our sorry hides."

"That's absolutely right," Fred reinforced the sentiment. "As far as Sister and I are concerned, the legend of hidden treasure is just that. Legend."

The Tanner sisters were good women, Hannah realized. Hard working and dedicated, with big, loving hearts. Loyal to a fault. They weren't protecting themselves; they were protecting Walker.

Hannah realized something else. Coming here, even under such dubious circumstances, had been the right thing for her. Hannah had known these women less than twenty-four hours, and yet, the three of them already shared a bond. It may have been born in crisis, but it went deeper than that. Oddly enough, she felt a kinship with these ladies that she lacked with her own mother. Sharing a secret only cemented that bond.

As crazy as it seemed—ghosts, goats, legends, and all—Hannah could see herself being happy here. Sadie and Fred would be her mentors, and Walker... well, she wasn't certain how Walker Jacoby fit into her future, but he would definitely be a part of it. Even if he weren't intricately tied to the town and its trust fund, he wasn't a man easily ignored.

She heard the lawyer's booted heel on the stairs now. Hannah slipped the letter out of sight.

"And who," she said softly, "doesn't love a good legend?"

Sadie beamed with pride and patted Hannah's arm. "We're so happy you were the one to buy our little town, dear. It was a risky move, putting all this history up for auction, but it couldn't have turned out better."

"Technically, *I* didn't buy the town," Hannah corrected. "It was my zany uncle, and his idea of a fun birthday present." She turned her gaze to the window, where she had a glimpse of the ram-shackled buildings beyond. When she first arrived, she thought JoeJoe had lost his mind, gifting her a rundown old town. Now she saw possibilities, and the opportunity of a fresh start.

"My uncle has given me a lot of presents over the years," she admitted. "I'll probably never admit this to him—not after some of the stunts he's pulled—but we're having a heart to heart, so I can tell you." She leaned in once again, her voice falling to a conspiratorial level.

"This gift," Hannah confided, her face softening with an affectionate smile, "may very well be the best one ever."

Thank you for visiting with us here in Hannah, Texas. We hope you'll come back soon!

Note from Author

Thank you for reading my book. I realize that without you, this would simply be a fun hobby. *With you*, I'm living my dream of being an author.

I know, I hate this part too, because it's like I'm asking you to bring a present to my own party. But if you enjoyed my tale, please take a moment to write a brief review on Amazon, Goodreads, and/or the platform of your choice. Reviews play such a pivotal role in an author's career. Reviews are how readers find us, how Amazon rates us, and how authors know if we're writing what *you* want to read.

After leaving your review, please feel free to drop me a personal note. I love visiting with readers! Here's how you can reach me:

beckiwillis.ccp@gmail.com

www.beckiwillis.com

https://www.facebook.com/beckiwillis.ccp/

ABOUT THE AUTHOR

Becki Willis, best known for her popular The Sisters, Texas Mystery Series and Forgotten Boxes, always dreamed of being an author. In November of '13, that dream became a reality. Since that time, she has published numerous books, won first place honors for Best Mystery Series, Best Suspense Fiction and Best Audio Book, and has introduced her imaginary friends to readers around the world.

An avid history buff, Becki likes to poke around in old places and learn about the past. Other addictions include reading, writing, junking, unraveling a good mystery, and coffee. She loves to travel, but believes coming home to her family and her Texas ranch is the best part of any trip. Becki is a member of the Association of Texas Authors, the National Association of Professional Women, and the Brazos Writers organization. She attended Texas A&M University and majored in Journalism.

Connect with Becki at http://www.beckiwillis.com/ and http://www.facebook.com/beckiwillis.ccp?ref=hl. Better yet, email her at beckiwillis.ccp@gmail.com. She loves to hear from readers and encourages feedback!